U0645825

图书在版编目(CIP)数据

中国故事:罗啻女儿回忆厦门生活:1851—1859/(美)玛丽·奥古斯塔·罗啻(Mary Augusta Doty)著;周维江,黄秀君译.—厦门:厦门大学出版社,2020.9
ISBN 978-7-5615-7857-5

Ⅰ.①中… Ⅱ.①玛… ②周… ③黄… Ⅲ.①回忆录—美国—现代 Ⅳ.①I712.55

中国版本图书馆 CIP 数据核字(2020)第 171920 号

出 版 人	郑文礼
责任编辑	章木良

出版发行	厦门大孝出版社
社　　址	厦门市软件园二期望海路 39 号
邮政编码	361008
总　　机	0592-2181111　0592-2181406(传真)
营销中心	0592-2184458　0592-2181365
网　　址	http://www.xmupress.com
邮　　箱	xmup@xmupress.com
印　　刷	厦门兴立通印刷设计有限公司

开本	720 mm×1 000 mm　1/16
印张	10.5
字数	170 千字
版次	2020 年 9 月第 1 版
印次	2020 年 9 月第 1 次印刷
定价	46.00 元

厦门大学出版社
微信二维码

厦门大学出版社
微博二维码

本书如有印装质量问题请直接寄承印厂调换

厦门社科丛书：

总 编 辑：中共厦门市委宣传部
　　　　　厦门市社会科学界联合会
执行编辑：厦门市社会科学院

编委会：

主　　任：李辉跃
副 主 任：潘少銮
委　　员：戴志望　　温金辉　　傅如荣　　纪　豪　　彭心安
　　　　　陈怀群　　庄志辉　　吴文祥　　李建发　　曾　路
　　　　　洪文建　　赵振祥　　陈　珍　　徐祥清　　王玉宗
　　　　　魏志坚　　李建钦　　陈振明　　朱　菁　　李　桢

编辑部：

主　　编：潘少銮
副 主 编：陈怀群　　庄志辉　　吴文祥　　王彦龙　　李　桢
编　　辑：李文泰

本书亦受厦门理工学院外国语学院译作资助项目资助

怎一个悲壮了得

——译者序

　　本书是罗啻（Elihu Doty，1809—1864）的女儿玛丽·罗啻（Mary Augusta Doty Smith）成年后回忆幼年时随父亲在厦门生活的故事。其中包括罗啻早年教育及南洋传教的经历、厦门见闻、时政事件（太平天国、克里米亚战争）、鼓浪屿散记、闽南人生活及风俗、编纂厦门话字典、著作翻译等。

　　罗啻是一位 19 世纪活跃于厦门的美国传教士和语言学家。1809 年 9 月 20 日生于纽约州的伯尔尼，入罗格斯学院立志学习商学，后转入新布伦瑞克神学院。他的第一任妻子是 1806 年出生于康涅狄格州华盛顿市利奇菲尔德的克拉丽莎·多利·阿克利（Clarissa D. Ackley）。受美部会（公理会海外宣教机构）委派，罗啻在 1836 年 6 月初偕夫人一起离开纽约前往南洋宣教。同年 9 月抵达荷属东印度爪哇的巴达维亚（今雅加达），展开为期 3 年的传教生活。[①] 当时的巴达维亚是伦敦公会的主要活动基地，罗啻在此学习了福建话。1838 年 10 月 15 日，罗啻经新加坡与波罗满（William J. Pohlman）牧师会合并一同前往婆罗洲，10 月 30 日经海路抵达三发，并改走陆路南下。11 月 24 日，抵达婆罗洲南部大城坤甸，随后于 27 日便走海路回新加坡。两人隔年再度来到坤甸，并在当地设置了传道站，开始学习广东话。[②]

　　1842 年，在厦门开拓传教工作的雅裨理（David Abeel）牧师在访问婆罗洲后，力荐罗啻与波罗满二人应前来人口众多的中国工作。1844 年 6 月 22 日，罗啻抵达厦门，起先在鼓浪屿宣教，后来才搬至厦门岛。抵达厦门后，罗啻积极学习厦门话，以笔记本记录新单字，编写成一本共 212 页的手册。然而，搬抵厦门不久，罗啻 6 岁的长子便去世。1845 年 10 月 5 日，罗啻的妻子也因染热病过世，年仅 39 岁，留下了两个女儿。早于一周之前，波罗满的夫人西奥多西娅（Mrs. Theodosia R. Scudder Pohlman）同样染病去世。③ 罗啻随后带着两家的孩子回美国交予亲戚朋友照料。他也借此机会在美国停留了一年半，到处分享在厦门的宣教工作与困难之处，希望引起教会的注目；在美期间，1847 年 2 月 17 日，他也与第二任妻子埃莉诺·奥古斯塔·史密斯·罗啻（Eleanor Augusta Smith Doty）相识并结婚。

1847 年 8 月 19 日，罗啻回到了厦门，与他同行的有约翰·打马字（John Van Nest Talmage）牧师。渐渐地，前来听道者渐增，罗啻、波罗满等人便在"新街仔"兴建一座礼拜堂，1848 年竣工，号称"中华第一圣堂"。但 1848 年 12 月 19 日，波罗满牧师在前往香港的途中遭遇海难，1849 年 2 月 11 日举行献堂礼仪式，亦同时追思波罗满。

1850 年，罗啻、打马字、养雅各（James H. Young）医生等人，为了宣教的需求，共同研拟出一套以拉丁字母连缀切音的白话字。1852 年，罗啻在养雅各医生的协助下，翻译了《约翰传福音书》，共 46 页，由大英圣书公会于广州出版，应当是第一部厦门音白话字的《圣经》译本。1854 年，罗啻将米怜（William Milne）的《乡训五十二则》翻译成白话字，并以《乡训十三则》为书名出版。④ 1853 年，罗啻于广州出版了以英语写成的教科书《翻译英华厦腔语汇》，这是最早期的闽南话教科书。⑤ 而罗啻在该书序言中提及大量参考了由已过世的波罗满牧师所采录的厦门话语汇。⑥ 尽管白话字的确切起源仍存有疑问，但一般都将罗啻与打马字一同认定为白话字的发明者，而这套文字系统至今仍是闽南话最常见的正写法。

1858 年 2 月 28 日，罗啻的第二任妻子埃莉诺去世。之后，罗啻与美部会解约，1859 年带子女返回美国。1861 年，他再度以美国归正教会宣教士的身份来到厦门工作，直到 1864 年 11 月退休为止。1865 年，罗啻在返回纽约的航程中于船上过世。

罗啻为人正直，品格完美，德才兼备，信念坚定，矢志不渝，具有强烈使命感和责任心，纵观其一生，怎一个悲壮了得。海外传教之路从来不是坦途，海路遥远，惊心动魄；宗教冲突引发杀戮，筚路蓝缕，荆棘坎坷；初入新境，风土人情迥异，水土不服，瘟疫流行，更可能是走上不归之路，但他义无反顾。他受美部会和归正会委派，先后于爪哇、婆罗洲及厦门等地从事传教工作长达 28 年，单单厦门就有 20 年。这期间，他接连遭受亡妻丧子之痛，频频受到打击，却依然百折不挠、坚韧固守。当时，厦门"热病"频现，病人忽冷忽热，周期性寒战、畏寒，发热，心悸，口渴，大汗淋漓，直到 19 世纪末，厦门海关医生曼逊（Patrick Manson）认定蚊子是疟原虫宿主，从而该病确诊为疟疾。[⑦]罗啻遭受的个人磨难更是匪夷所思。1844 年 6 月 24 日，罗啻和波罗满各自偕家眷自婆罗洲第一次抵达厦门后不久，两个家庭就经历了失去亲人的痛苦。抵达厦门仅 26 天，1844 年 7 月 19 日罗啻 6 岁的儿子费里斯（Ferris Holmes Doty）就染病夭折。一年后，波罗满牧师也失去了 2 岁的儿子爱德华（Edward Joseph Pohlman）。1845 年 9 月 30 日，波罗满妻子西奥多西娅身染热病，刚生下一个婴儿后数小时就一同去世，终年 34 岁。一星期之后的 10 月 5 日，罗啻妻子克拉丽莎也去世了，终年 39 岁。1847 年，罗啻再婚后马上返华，但不幸接踵而至。1848 年 7 月 14 日罗啻 7 个月大的男婴爱德华（Edward Smith Doty）夭折，1858 年 2 月 28 日第二任妻子埃莉诺去世。1858 年 7 月 2 日，罗啻牧师 4 个月大的女婴埃尔迈拉（Elmira Louisa Doty）夭折。同年末，波罗满牧师海难去世，罗啻痛失同道好友。次年初，罗啻不得不乘船再次踏上返美旅程，把孩子们安顿在岳父母和朋友们的身边。在厦门，罗啻两次丧妻并失去三个孩子，但是重重打击没有击倒罗啻，历经家国沧桑、教会变迁，他仍义无反顾，1861 年再次只身三赴厦门，直至 1864 年 11 月体力明显日渐不支才退休为止。1865 年 3 月 18 日返程途中船舶到港靠岸之前的 4 天，逝世于船上。

罗啻精益求精，秉持坦率、审慎、自由之精神；他勤劳、坚定，性格沉稳，不浮夸，鞠躬尽瘁，死而后已；面对困难，他展现出平静的英雄主义，其身上体现出清教徒隐忍、坚韧、百折不挠的精神，虽命运多舛，但历久弥坚。其一生可谓悲哉！壮哉！可为一叹！

提请读者注意的是：本书是作者玛丽·罗啻成年后的回忆录，囿于事发之际年岁太轻，因此无法按照先后顺序来叙述事件，致使故事的跳跃性较大；又鉴于其参考母亲的信件或他人讲述补足缺失信息，较年幼时更全面地弄清一些情况，但是作者自陈不能保证信息完全正确，尤其是人生初年的事情，多为追忆、补忆。故此，细节模糊、可疑处译者在文中添加注释提醒，至于历史的考证尚待推敲处，请读者审慎自鉴。

鉴于作者并未按照时间顺序、事件关联度而安排写作，全文条理性不够令人满意。为方便读者厘清脉络，译者依据主观判断，在原文已有的少量带方括号的标题之外，自行添加章节目录一统全文，寄望于恰中肯綮，奢祈免于画蛇添足、狗尾续貂之嫌。笔者自担其责。

值此译作付梓出版之际，译者深怀感恩之心，回顾过去一年中所得到的无私关怀与帮助。感谢厦门同文书库给予立项支持，厦门市社会科学院陈夏晗女士和李文泰先生的协调与指导；厦门理工学院闽南文化海外传播研究基地的支持以及基地同事的建议与批评；尤其是集美大学苏宗文教授亲自为本书审校，答疑解惑，无私奉献。更值得一提的是，厦门地方文史专家叶克豪先生拨冗通读译稿，提出审阅意见，指出翻译不当、历史失实之处，对先生提携后辈的高风亮节、精益求精的学术精神，感怀至深，无以言表。唯有以一丝不苟、严谨治学的态度，聊以为报。还要感谢厦门大学出版社章木良编辑的团队，水平专业、快速高效地解决原稿中存在的内容与形式上的诸多问题。最后，对所有关心、关爱本书的朋友、同事，在此不具名地一并致谢。

周维江
2020 年 7 月

【参考文献】

① Bruggink, D J, Baker, K N. By Grace Alone: Stories of the Reformed Church in America [M]. Grand Rapids: Wm. B. Eerdmans. 2004: 92.

② 赖永祥.赖永祥讲书——罗啻牧师[EB/OL]. http://www.laijohn.com/works/kangsu/07.htm.

③ 叶克豪.鼓浪屿内厝澳崎仔尾传教士公墓文献考证[M]//鼓浪屿研究：第8辑.北京：社会科学文献出版社，2018: 161.

④ Wylie, A. Rev. Elihu Doty and His Publications [EB/OL]. http://www.laijohn.com/archiv es/pm/Doty,E/biog/wylie.htm.

⑤ Klöter, H. A History of Peh-oe-ji[EB/OL]. http://210.240.194.97/ungian/POJ/siausit/2002/2002POJGTH/lunbun/K2-kloeter.htm.

⑥ Doty E. Introduction, Anglo-Chinese Manual with Romanized Colloquial in the Amoy Dialect [M]. Canton: Samuel Wells Williams, 1853.

⑦ 叶克豪.鼓浪屿内厝澳崎仔尾传教士公墓文献考证[M]//鼓浪屿研究：第8辑.北京：社会科学文献出版社，2018: 161.

目 录
Contents

第一章　早年经历
Chapter 1　Early Life Experience ································· *1*

教育背景与爪哇遇挫
Education, Java Frustrations ····························· *1*

痛失妻与子
Loss of Kindred ······································· *3*

再婚
Remarriage ·· *4*

哀伤的婚礼
A Sad Wedding ······································· *7*

再度出发
Setting out ·· *7*

抵达厦门
Arrival at Amoy ······································ *10*

第二章　厦门生活之一
Chapter 2　Life in Amoy（1） ························· *14*

通信今夕
Communication Then and Now ······················· *14*

时局：太平天国起义
Tide：Taiping Rebellion ······························· *15*

来自家乡的箱子
Boxes from Home ···································· *17*

大桶黄油
Hogsheads of Butter ·· 19

顽皮的熊孩子
Naughty MKs ··· 20

我们的房子
Our House ··· 21

第三章　厦门生活之二
Chapter 3　Life in Amoy（2）·· 27

7月4日的国庆聚会
4th of July Party ··· 27

英国朋友及克里米亚战争
English Friends & the Crimean War ·· 28

鼓浪屿的第一架钢琴
Gulangyu's First Piano ·· 30

与军人交往：佩里准将访问厦门
Association with Navy Officers: Commodore Perry
Visited Amoy ·· 31

原罪：小孩儿撒谎
Original Sin：Lying ·· 32

异端邪说?
Heretics ? ··· 34

耐心与呵护
Patience and Loving Care ⋯⋯⋯⋯⋯⋯⋯⋯⋯⋯⋯⋯⋯⋯⋯⋯⋯⋯⋯ 34

糖果故事
Candy Stories ⋯⋯⋯⋯⋯⋯⋯⋯⋯⋯⋯⋯⋯⋯⋯⋯⋯⋯⋯⋯⋯⋯⋯ 36

剃头匠
The Barber ⋯⋯⋯⋯⋯⋯⋯⋯⋯⋯⋯⋯⋯⋯⋯⋯⋯⋯⋯⋯⋯⋯⋯⋯ 38

每日菜单
Daily Menu ⋯⋯⋯⋯⋯⋯⋯⋯⋯⋯⋯⋯⋯⋯⋯⋯⋯⋯⋯⋯⋯⋯⋯⋯ 39

第四章　鼓浪屿散记
Chapter 4　Random Notes of Gulangyu ⋯⋯⋯⋯⋯⋯⋯⋯⋯⋯⋯⋯⋯ 44

乐在鼓浪屿
Fun on Gulangyu ⋯⋯⋯⋯⋯⋯⋯⋯⋯⋯⋯⋯⋯⋯⋯⋯⋯⋯⋯⋯⋯ 44

孟加拉虎
Bengal Tiger ⋯⋯⋯⋯⋯⋯⋯⋯⋯⋯⋯⋯⋯⋯⋯⋯⋯⋯⋯⋯⋯⋯⋯ 45

父亲的陪伴
Father's Company ⋯⋯⋯⋯⋯⋯⋯⋯⋯⋯⋯⋯⋯⋯⋯⋯⋯⋯⋯⋯⋯ 46

拜访领事
Consuls Visited ⋯⋯⋯⋯⋯⋯⋯⋯⋯⋯⋯⋯⋯⋯⋯⋯⋯⋯⋯⋯⋯⋯ 47

罗啻领事
Consul Doty ⋯⋯⋯⋯⋯⋯⋯⋯⋯⋯⋯⋯⋯⋯⋯⋯⋯⋯⋯⋯⋯⋯⋯ 48

鼓浪屿传教士公墓
Gulangyu Cemetery ⋯⋯⋯⋯⋯⋯⋯⋯⋯⋯⋯⋯⋯⋯⋯⋯⋯⋯⋯⋯ 49

"勇士"号军舰来访
"Man of War" ·· 50

纽扣和寺庙
Buttons & the Temple ······································ 51

中国人家内部
Chinese Interiors ··· 52

雨中的舢板
Sampans in the Rain ······································ 54

许多国家的船只
Ships of Many Nations ···································· 55

帕西人
Parsees ··· 58

中国访客
Chinese Visitors ··· 59

写家书
Writing Letters Home ····································· 62

母亲的挚友
Mrs. Boyd & Mrs. Syme ····································· 63

第一次厦门国际基督教团契
The First XICF—Xiamen International Christian
Fellowship ·· 65

第五章　父母的成就、孩子的成长和当地的习俗
Chapter 5　Accomplishments of Parents, Growth of Kids, and Local Customs ·············· 69

《翻译英华厦腔语汇》
Amoy Dictionary ·············· 69

女子教育
Women's Education ··············· 71

重建"晨星"号
Rebuilding the "Morning Star" ·············· 74

信号山与邮船
Signal Hill; Mail Ships ·············· 75

隔离检疫：童年的第一个悲伤
Quarantine: First Childhood Sorrow ··············· 76

孩子戏
Childhood Dramatics ·············· 77

吃杧果
Eating Mangoes ·············· 80

回国上学计划；母亲和朋友之死
Plans for American Education; Mother & Friend's Death ················ 82

我最后一个与母亲共度的生日
My Last Birthday with Mom ·············· 84

送王船
Annual Spectacle: Sacrifice-offering to Sea-god ·············· 89

缠足
Footbinding ·············· 89

第六章　归程
Chapter 6　Journey Back to America ⋯⋯⋯⋯⋯⋯⋯⋯⋯⋯⋯⋯⋯⋯⋯⋯ *95*

母亲去世
Mother's Death ⋯⋯⋯⋯⋯⋯⋯⋯⋯⋯⋯⋯⋯⋯⋯⋯⋯⋯⋯⋯⋯⋯⋯⋯ *95*

没娘的孩子有人管
Auntie Talmage, Mr. Rapaljo ⋯⋯⋯⋯⋯⋯⋯⋯⋯⋯⋯⋯⋯⋯⋯⋯⋯ *97*

打点行囊
Packing up ⋯⋯⋯⋯⋯⋯⋯⋯⋯⋯⋯⋯⋯⋯⋯⋯⋯⋯⋯⋯⋯⋯⋯⋯⋯ *98*

晕船
Seasickness ⋯⋯⋯⋯⋯⋯⋯⋯⋯⋯⋯⋯⋯⋯⋯⋯⋯⋯⋯⋯⋯⋯⋯⋯⋯ *102*

船上宠物梦
Dream of Pets ⋯⋯⋯⋯⋯⋯⋯⋯⋯⋯⋯⋯⋯⋯⋯⋯⋯⋯⋯⋯⋯⋯⋯⋯ *103*

途中
en Route ⋯⋯⋯⋯⋯⋯⋯⋯⋯⋯⋯⋯⋯⋯⋯⋯⋯⋯⋯⋯⋯⋯⋯⋯⋯⋯⋯ *105*

船长的宠物猴
Captain's Pet Monkey ⋯⋯⋯⋯⋯⋯⋯⋯⋯⋯⋯⋯⋯⋯⋯⋯⋯⋯⋯⋯ *107*

水手与乘务员
Sailor and Stewardess ⋯⋯⋯⋯⋯⋯⋯⋯⋯⋯⋯⋯⋯⋯⋯⋯⋯⋯⋯⋯ *108*

由南向北
Sailing North ⋯⋯⋯⋯⋯⋯⋯⋯⋯⋯⋯⋯⋯⋯⋯⋯⋯⋯⋯⋯⋯⋯⋯⋯ *110*

赤道无风带
The Doldrums ⋯⋯⋯⋯⋯⋯⋯⋯⋯⋯⋯⋯⋯⋯⋯⋯⋯⋯⋯⋯⋯⋯⋯⋯ *113*

前方有陆地
Land Ahead ⋯⋯⋯⋯⋯⋯⋯⋯⋯⋯⋯⋯⋯⋯⋯⋯⋯⋯⋯⋯⋯⋯⋯⋯⋯ *114*

回家
Going Home ⋯⋯⋯⋯⋯⋯⋯⋯⋯⋯⋯⋯⋯⋯⋯⋯⋯⋯⋯⋯⋯⋯⋯⋯ *117*

只吃米饭!
Rice—Nothing Else! ⋯⋯⋯⋯⋯⋯⋯⋯⋯⋯⋯⋯⋯⋯⋯⋯⋯⋯⋯ *121*

小姨妈
Aunt Mary ⋯⋯⋯⋯⋯⋯⋯⋯⋯⋯⋯⋯⋯⋯⋯⋯⋯⋯⋯⋯⋯⋯⋯⋯ *122*

第三文化的孩子
Third Culture Kids ⋯⋯⋯⋯⋯⋯⋯⋯⋯⋯⋯⋯⋯⋯⋯⋯⋯⋯⋯ *124*

父亲返华
Back to China ⋯⋯⋯⋯⋯⋯⋯⋯⋯⋯⋯⋯⋯⋯⋯⋯⋯⋯⋯⋯⋯ *126*

外祖母写信
Grandmother's Letter Writing ⋯⋯⋯⋯⋯⋯⋯⋯⋯⋯⋯ *128*

邮件和父亲离世
Mail & Doty's Death ⋯⋯⋯⋯⋯⋯⋯⋯⋯⋯⋯⋯⋯⋯⋯⋯⋯ *130*

附录　族谱中的罗奋
Appendix　Doty in The Doty–Doten Family in America ⋯⋯⋯⋯⋯ *135*

第一章　早年经历

Chapter 1　Early Life Experience

教育背景与爪哇遇挫

我的父亲罗啻，1809年出生于纽约州的伯尔尼，就学于罗格斯学院，现今的新泽西大学。他同时从新泽西州的新布伦瑞克神学院获得学位，并于1836年赴印尼爪哇岛传教。

传教的新使命尚处于初始阶段，然而在缅甸、印度、桑威奇群岛（今称夏威夷群岛）传教肇始，尽管筚路蓝缕，充满血腥和杀戮，频吃闭门羹，但是成效慢慢显现。当那一小批不屈不挠的英雄号召更多帮手，接替他们并扩大队伍时，故乡的一些人心潮澎湃，准备接受挑战。

救世主发出基督教走向全世界的"最后命令"，使得教徒们纷纷想到日本、中国，还有太平洋诸岛；带着威严与急迫，这一

Education, Java Frustrations

My father, Elihu Doty (born at Berne, N.Y., in 1809), received his course of instruction at Rutgers College, now known as the University of New Jersey: he also graduated from the Theological Seminary there, and in 1836 went out to the Island of Java, as a missionary.

This new work was in its infancy, but facts of its beginnings in Burma, India, and the Sandwich Islands (known today as the Hawaiian Group) which told of hardships and cruelties and killings and shut doors, had drifted in, and calls for helpers to take their places and to increase their forces, came from the little band of heroes who never gave up, which thrilled the hearts of some in the Homeland to accept the challenge.

While the "Last Command" of our Saviour to go into all the world, stirred thoughts of Japan and China and the "Islands of the Sea"; and it became a vivid reality, imperative in its Authority.

Father took his course of study with this objective in view. The Dutch Reformed Church was beginning missionary work in Java, and he found a woman of high heart and brave spirit in Clarissa Ackley, to accompany him.

There are some writings which tell of difficulties and opposition from native priests, and disappointments, which they tried to overcome, in face of danger to the lives of two other companions also, who had joined him later.

After three years, he turned to Borneo—the Dutch Reformed Church thinking their own Holland Church would be respected by the Dutch Government, and settled there.

But instead, it joined the opposition and closed its doors to missionary work; and again, father and his wife and little son, went out—this time to Amoy, China, having heard through Chinese who had found their way to Borneo in trade, that there was a more kindly feeling there, in parts of the land. Among the very earliest names I remember hearing, is that of Bishop Boone, who evidently became a valued friend of these new adventurers in the land of his choice too, in Missionary Work of the Episcopal Church, not a great distance from them, where work still carries his

命令变成清晰的现实。

父亲怀着这样的目标开始课程学习。美国荷兰归正教会 ① 当时正着手向爪哇派遣差会，而且父亲遇到了可以与之同行的女子——勇敢刚毅的克拉丽莎·阿克利。

当地教士对他们加以阻挠与抵制的故事，以及他们面对后来加入的两个伙伴面临生命危险时必须要克服的失望情绪，都有所记述。

三年后，由于荷兰归正教会认为他们自己的荷兰教会将会得到荷兰政府的认可，于是父亲转到婆罗洲，并定居于此。

但是，事与愿违，教会反而中止了父亲在婆罗洲的差传任务，将父亲指派到别处；父亲带着妻子和年幼的儿子又一次踏上征程，这次是前往中国厦门，他们听来到婆罗洲做贸易的中国商人说，中国的部分地区对传教士态度较为友好。我记得我最早听到过的人名中，有一个叫文主教 ② 的人，他为美国圣公会工作。在这片充满志同道合人士的土地上，他无疑是新来探险者难得的助力，距离我父母的教会不远处就是圣公会的场所，时至今日仍然以文主教的名誉布道，以示纪念。

在厦门的这一小伙人打下了坚实的基础，开局良好。

痛失妻与子

然而，悲伤与负累接踵而至。先是他幼子，然后是他妻子相继去世，留下两个小女儿 ③ 要照看。同时，传教士 ④ 中另有两个孩子成了孤儿，所以父亲决定带着四个孩子启程回国，航期六个月，父亲既当爹又当妈。

1846年或1847年，父亲一行人抵达纽约。亲戚们领养了另外两个孤儿，海外差传教士的热心朋友们主动提出收养和照顾他的两个女儿。

海外差传团的这伙朋友们觉得，当务之急是：像我父亲这样既能胜任，又愿意并恳求重新回到厦门同事们身边的人，就该付诸行动。

孩子们和父亲很亲，这从书信中可见一斑。重返厦门意味着与深爱的孩子们分开，但父亲承受分离之痛，并做好返华准备。

父亲一生中，总是把"人类灵魂深处

name memorially.

The little force in Amoy were able to lay good foundations, and the beginnings prospered.

Loss of Kindred

Sorrows and burdens followed him. His baby, and then his wife died, and there were two little girls left to his care. At the same time, two other little children of the mission were left orphans, and it was decided that father should undertake the six months' voyage with the four children, being father and mother both to them.

In 1846 or '47, he arrived in New York City. Relatives claimed the other two, and warm friends of Foreign Missions offered to care for his little ones by adoption.

It seemed imperative to the band of friends of the new missions, that one so ably fitted as father was, and so wanted and begged to return to his few associates in Amoy, should do so.

He accepted the sacrifice of parting from his dearly loved children (probed by writings which show how close they were to him) and prepared to return to China.

Always during his life, "the Voice of God in the Soul of Man" was to him a personal and living fact, calling for first loyalty and obedience, and directing of his course through great decisions and great burdens, great sorrows and great joys.

In the meantime, while in the Homeland, he preached in many pulpits—disseminating knowledge of this new work and needs, and seeking to create interest in the same.

神的声音"视为针对他个人的，而且又那么真切，并呼唤他尽可能地忠诚与顺服，指引他经历大试炼、大担当、大悲痛、大欢乐。

其间，趁回国之机，他去许多讲坛布道，让海外传教的新任务和要求为人所知，试图引起人们的兴趣。

Remarriage

再　婚

During this time, he met my mother, who responded to his desire that they should marry and return with him to Amoy.

My mother, Eleanor Augusta Smith, born 1822 in Troy, New Jersey, the daughter of Hiram and Mary A. Smith, was the oldest of six brothers and three sisters, a most beloved member of the large family, holding an influential and responsible place in the economy of the daily, busy life on a large prosperous farm. She was also a leading and loved member of the community.

It was a great event when it was decided that she should have the advantage of a year at boarding school as her mother enjoyed before her, appreciating its value in forming character and adding graces to a beautiful young girl's

正是这段时间，父亲和我母亲相遇了。父亲希望他们结婚后一起返回厦门，母亲同意了。

我的母亲，埃莉诺·奥古斯塔·史密斯，1822年出生于新泽西州的特洛伊城，在海勒姆·史密斯和玛丽·史密斯所生六子三女中排行老大。在这个大家庭中，人人都喜爱她，家里的农场很大、很兴隆，在操持每日繁忙的家务事上，她的地位举足轻重、责任重大。在社区生活中，她也是让人爱戴的领袖人物。

下面这个决定事关重大。母亲决定利用一年的时间读寄宿学校，就像外祖母以前那样，借此磨炼性格，并给她碧玉桃李的人生阶段增添魅力。但是，这在那时代价颇大，因为不仅仅牵涉到金钱，还牵涉到她不得不放弃指导和帮助年少的弟弟、妹妹，她对家长来说可是难得的帮手。但家长十分愉快而又主动地出钱，母亲于是去了宾夕法尼亚州的伯利恒⑤，像外祖母一样，就读于时至今日依然兴盛的摩拉维亚神学院。等到一年后返回时，母亲已然出落成小伙子们青睐不已的窈窕淑女，最终当父亲有一次在她家附近宣教时，二人相遇了。他们的关系从相识相知，发展到让母亲愿意在海外传教的大冒险中追随父亲，生死与共。

母亲家收到多方来信，为父亲的品德和能力，以及在教职中拥有的名望背书。还有一位了解和见证过父亲是如何为人夫、为人父的人，写了封推荐信，介绍父亲具有的幸福家庭生活所需的那些可爱品质。由于与父亲相识时间短暂，这些正面肯定此时给了母亲些许安慰。

不过，反对的声音也是有的。关于人们在未知世界四处传教所经历的恐怖故事的记述，让母亲的家人和朋友强烈反对母

life. But it involved great expense for those days, not only in money, but in foregoing her valuable assistance in guiding and helping the younger brothers and sisters. But it was gladly and willingly given to her and she went—to the still flourishing Moravian Seminary at Bethlehem, Pennsylvania, where her mother went before her—and returned after the year, a young lady, to receive the marked attention of many young men, and in course of time met my father during one of this preaching services near her home, and the acquaintance ripened into readiness to throw in her lot with him in the Great Adventure.

Letters from many sources were received, endorsing father's character and abilities, and high standing in his chosen work. There came also a testimonial from one who had known and seen him as husband and father, as to lovable qualities so desirable in making a happy home life, and these assurances about one whose acquaintance was a short one, gave some comfort at this time.

But O! The opposition that developed! The accounts of terrible experiences of the band of men and women here and there in the unknown world, filled members of the family and friends with strong objections against it, notwithstanding father's assurances that conditions were much ameliorated in established centers where there were missions. And she was so needed at home—the eldest of the brothers and sisters, whose influence for all that was pure and good could not be spared; and there was the disparity in their ages—he, thirty-nine; she, twenty-five.

When it looked as if all resources of persuasion at home were to fail, brother John, the next younger to Samuel, at Yale College, wrote to him that it looked as if Eleanor intended to marry that man from China, and that he had better come home, and quickly, to stop it! He had always been able to influence and advise his loved sister, with whom there was a peculiarly close bond of sympathetic understanding and taste, and had often persuaded her from hers to his own will; and he did come at once. But he found her adamant this time! Then "old Jack" took a hand. He was a left-over from slave days in the Northern states, and had always remained as a member of the household. He pleaded with her not to go. She had always obeyed her mother, and she should do so now, and he couldn't stand it to have her go—then reversed his plea into begging her to take him along to take care of her, if she wouldn't give it up. And when she showed him her purpose, in despair, he

亲与其同行，尽管父亲保证说：在已经建立的传教点，条件已大为改善。反对还来自家里需要她，作为老大，她对弟弟妹妹们有着纯净、良好的影响，无可替代。反对还来自父母的年龄差距，父亲时年39岁，母亲才25岁。

当所有的劝阻方法似乎都将失效时，在耶鲁学院⑥读书的大哥塞缪尔收到二弟约翰的信。信中说，大姐看起来打算与从中国回来的那个家伙结婚，大哥最好马上回来一趟，阻止他们。在以往，塞缪尔和大姐特别地灵犀相通、品位相投，关系密切，他总能影响自己钟爱的大姐，给她出谋划策，而且通常能劝说大姐同意他的想法。大哥立马就回来了，但他却发现大姐这回固执己见，不肯让步！于是，老杰克出手了。杰克是北方诸州奴隶制时代的遗民，一直是家中一员。他请求母亲不要去。母亲总是很听外祖母的话，这回也应该一样才对，她真走的话，杰克受不了。继而，杰克又把恳求换成乞求，如果她坚持离家的话，那就带上他去照顾她。当母亲向杰克讲明自己的任务后，绝望中，杰克买了一瓶毒药，想要结束自己的生命。幸好被外祖母及时发现，把毒药夺走，并严厉批评他，才让杰克从狂乱中平息下来。

【哀伤的婚礼】⑦

最终，父母的婚礼在教堂中举行。这座教堂，是母亲孩提、少女、青年时期的兴趣和关注所在，这是那些早期日子里的风俗，同时也是教会与社区之间的联系。在各处聚来的朋友和亲戚的聆听下，典礼隆重肃穆，但弥漫着忧伤的气息。海外传教被视为等同于死亡，当然还有各种痛苦，而见证这场注定她一生命运的婚礼足以让人充满忧伤，因为他们社区的一位年轻美丽的姑娘将要转身离去，蹈火赴汤。

再度出发

父母在国内逗留了约一个月，然后不得不辞别。外祖父送他们到波士顿，他们的船"赫伯"号停泊于此。

在波士顿，母亲给家乡的亲人们买了

bought a dose of poison with which he intended to end his life, but was discovered in time by grandmother, who took it away from him and sternly calmed his frenzy!

〔A Sad Wedding〕

So, in course of time, they were married in the church where so many of her interests through childhood, girlhood, and young womanhood were centered, as was the custom in those earlier days, in relationships between Church and Community. A solemn, sad ceremony, listened to by friends and kindred from far and near, was performed. For the going into this Service was looked upon as about equivalent to death, certainly to all kinds of distresses; and to witness the ceremony that was to bind her to this life, was enough to fill everyone with sadness, that a beautiful young woman of their community was about to enter upon, and separate herself from them all in doing it.

Setting out

Father and mother remained in this country about one month and then farewells had to be said. Her father accompanied them to Boston where their ship "Heber" was anchored.

8

From there she purchased little mementoes to be taken back to loved ones—a tiny cushion of pretty white satin with pink flowers on it, a baby thing, was sent to "Little Sister Molly", only three years old—the baby often in her arms took as well as in her mother's—and so peculiarly dear. This tiny cushion has always been kept as a sacred treasure; and only lately, at eighty-five years of age, she passed it on to another Molly, who I hope will give it tender care for all it meant—to the one who first selected it, and sent it to her baby sister of three, —and remember the emotions which must have accompanied the gift, for "auld lang syne."

The Mission Board in Boston, under whom they were to serve, asked for their daguerreotypes, to put with their collection of missionaries, which was done; and long years after, this same little sister Molly (as she often was spoken of in returning letters from mother) was in Boston and inquired at the Mission Rooms if it could be possible there was a picture of her sister, not knowing any had been taken, though she knew others were in their keeping. There was search for the box of pictures of the earliest days, and the top layers of daguerreotypes were opened to no purpose, so on and on they went until nearly all had been scanned. Only the bottom layer remained of those earliest pictures, and not many of them. One more was taken

些小纪念品，其中送给小妹莫利的是婴儿玩具小垫子，漂亮的白色锦缎上绣着粉红色花朵。莫利仅仅3岁，格外招人爱，母亲和外祖母经常抱着她。莫利一直把小垫子当作圣洁的宝贝珍藏，直到最近85岁时，把它传给家族中的下一个莫利。我希望小莫利能够好好珍惜它，为了那最初挑选和赠送礼物的人；并记得礼物所蕴含的情义，为了"昔日好时光"。

父母为之效力的波士顿差会曾向他们要过银版⑧照片，以便收录到已经完成的传教士集子里。多年之后，还是那个小妹莫利（母亲在回信中也经常提到她），有一次来到波士顿，在差会收藏室询问是否可能存有她姐姐的照片，尽管她知道差会保存了别人的照片，但不肯定姐姐是否照过相。他们开始翻找早年的照片，放在上层的照片被漫无目的地翻了一通，翻来翻去差点全部翻找完毕。只有底层保存着最早期的照片，数量不多。又一张照片抽出来了，莫利一下子充满了震惊和激动，照片中的人仿佛鲜活地展现在她面前，竟然是我母亲和父亲的合影，正像她依稀记得的

1847年2月17日结婚的罗奢夫妇
（作者在本书中提到的银版照片）

out—and, with a shock and thrill, almost as if a living presence had appeared, were sister Eleanor and father taken together, just as the little girl of three dimly recalled her—sad faces, yet strong and calm, and ready to accept their appointed Mission. (I have a photograph of it, framed and hanging over my desk.)

Soon they embarked on the "good ship 'Heber'" for a six month's voyage around the Horn and over the Pacific. A young man (brother of the noted Dr. Dewitt Talmadge [Talmage], of a long and influential service in the Metropolitan pulpit) had joined the Amoy Mission, and he was a passenger on the "Heber", too.

These, having the same common heart interests, became warm friends, and the new ones began intensive study of the Chinese language under the tutelage of father.

Arrival at Amoy

And so, with no "undue course of events" to mar their journey, they arrived at a port of entry in China and were transferred to a smaller coast vessel and taken to Amoy, where the small band of missionaries awaiting their arrival gave them a loving and cordial welcome.

This first year was one full of new experiences, not the least of which was the birth of their first

样子：没有笑容，但很坚定、冷静，随时待命。（我复制了这张照片，装裱起来，挂在书桌上方。）

不久之后，父母登上"赫伯"号，开启为时六个月、绕过合恩角、横跨太平洋的航程。同船而行的还有一个年轻人[9]，也加入厦门传教中来，他是狄维特·打马字博士[10]的哥哥。狄维特在纽约大都会讲坛布道已久，影响颇大，负有盛名。

由于内心志趣相投，这一行人成为好朋友，新手们还在父亲的指导下开始汉语强化学习。

抵达厦门

于是，一路上没有什么波折，顺风顺水地到达中国入境口岸，换乘较小的登岸船只，被送到了厦门。这里，一小队传教士正等着他们，热烈而又衷心地欢迎他们到来。

初到厦门的第一年全部是新体验，其中包括他们的第一个孩子出生。爱德华·史密斯·罗啻出生几个月后夭折，这是母亲辞别一众家人和朋友后要面对的第一个严峻考验。

离家之前，母亲曾告诉外祖母她怀孕的事；怀孕的日子里没有外祖母精心的现场指导，母亲一个人面对所有初为人母的经历；1848年，掩埋了自己的第一个孩子。外祖母一直揪着的心又添新痛，因为她和家中至亲们认识到他们亲爱的孩子面前还有许多严峻的考验，而这个孩子的一切遭遇，他们几个月里都无从知晓。

baby, Edward Smith Doty, who died when a few months old—the first deep trial to meet mother, after the farewells had been spoken with the loved home circle and friends.

She had told her mother of the great fact, before she left; and faced all the new maternal experiences, without the loving guiding presence most wanted during such weeks and months; and then laid her first born away, in 1848. And, also, the mother heart left behind held an added ache, as she and the others of the closely-knit home circle recognized the many serious possibilities lying before their precious child, of which they could know nothing for many months.

【注释】

① 美国归正教会可以溯源到荷兰母会，起初其会众多为荷裔。其名称也经历过变化。教会长期使用的名称是"北美洲荷兰新教归正教会"（The Reformed protestant Dutch Church of North America）；1819 年改称"美国荷兰归正教会"（The Dutch Reformed Church in the America），罗啻正是处于这一时段，所以书中提到教会时常用的英文是"The Dutch Reformed Church"；1867 年脱离荷兰母会后才正式称为"美国归正教会"（The Reformed Church in America）。参见：杨丽，叶克豪.美国归正教在厦门[M].台北：龙图腾文化公司，2013: 25.——译者注

② 文主教，即文惠廉（William Jones Boone, 1811—1864），美国卡罗莱纳州人，原攻读法律，为传教而改习医学并获医学博士学位。1834年5月，美国圣公会差会决定以中国为布道区。1837年7月，文惠廉偕妻子暂寓新加坡，学习汉语，熟悉中国风土人情，并尝试向当地华人传教。1837年，到爪哇的华人中间传教。1842年鸦片战争后，先后于澳门、香港逗留，1842年2月7日搭乘一艘英国海军"澳大利亚人"号舰艇离开香港前往厦门，于2月24日上午在鼓浪屿登岸。但不幸的是，文惠廉牧师娘萨拉（Sarah Amelia Boone）逗留了不到3个月，因患流行热病，于8月30日去世。1843年春天，文惠廉牧师带着两个孩子和一个鼓浪屿小佣人黄光彩也离开鼓浪屿回国。1844年5月

24日，文惠廉牧师在上海开辟了美国圣公会新的传教工场，先在老城厢研习上海方言，传教并主持洗礼仪式，继则扩大布道。1845年，在虹口头坝一带租地造屋设堂。1848年，文惠廉向清苏松太道提出将虹口辟为美侨居留地（后称美租界）。1853年，圣公会第一所有堂宇建筑的救主堂在百老汇路、蓬路（即文监师路，今塘沽路）路口落成，是上海吴淞江北建立最早的教堂。1852年与1857年，文惠廉两次回美国，率领一批新传教士重来上海。活动地域扩大至嘉定、苏州、无锡和青浦等地。1864年7月，文惠廉在上海病逝，中华圣公会史称其为"创立教会之第一人"。后来美国圣公会在武昌所办的大学也以他的姓氏命名，即"Boone University"（文华大学）。文惠廉的长子文恒理（Henry William Boone，1839—1925）是传教医生，1880年创办了上海同仁医院（St. Luke's Hospital）。次子小文惠廉（William Jones Boone，Jr.，1846—1891）1846年生于上海，1884年接任美国圣公会江苏教区主教，1891年在上海去世。——译者注

③ 首任妻子克拉丽莎·阿克利育有三子，由于长子费里斯·罗啻（Ferris Doty）于1844年7月19日在厦门去世，此时留下长女克拉丽莎（Clarissa Doty）及次女阿梅莉亚（Amelia Doty）。——译者注

④ 1844年6月24日，罗啻牧师偕牧师娘克拉丽莎·阿克利和孩子，以及波罗满牧师（Rev. William Pohlman）偕牧师娘西奥多西娅（Theodosia R. Scudder Pohlman）和孩子自婆罗洲抵达厦门。两家人起初住在鼓浪屿，不久迁至厦门寮仔后靠海的较舒适的住所。一所商行经过改建之后成为他们的住所，罗啻牧师一家住在楼上，波罗满牧师一家住在楼下。从一开始，两个家庭就经历了失去亲人的痛苦。抵达厦门仅26天，罗啻牧师6岁的儿子费里斯就染病死了。一年后，波罗满牧师也失去了2岁的儿子爱德华（Edward Joseph Pohlman）。1845年9月30日，波罗满牧师娘西奥多西娅身染热病，生下一个婴儿后数小时就与婴儿一同去世，终年34岁。一星期之后的10月5日，罗啻牧师娘克拉丽莎也去世了，终年39岁。他们都安卧在内厝澳崎仔尾坟场文惠廉牧师娘的周旁。他们的死因全都是染上热病——疟疾，直到19世纪末，厦门海关医生曼逊（Dr. Patrick Manson）认定蚊子是疟原虫宿主，之后才证实了数十年未解的热病是经由蚊子叮咬而传播的疟疾。[参考叶克豪：《鼓浪屿内厝澳崎仔尾传教士公墓文献考证》，《鼓浪屿研究（第八辑）》，北京：社会科学文献出版社，2018年，第161页]——译者注

⑤ 伯利恒，美国宾夕法尼亚州东部一个城市，位于费城西北偏北的利哈依河畔，是一个重要的钢铁生产中心。——译者注

⑥ 耶鲁学院是耶鲁大学在1718—1887年间的正式名称。现在则指耶鲁大学的本科部分，由12所寄宿制学院构成，每个学院是以校史人物、地点或知名校

友命名。每个本科生都有归属学院。——译者注

⑦ 加【】的标题为原书所有，未加【】的标题为译者整理添加。——译者注

⑧ Daguerreotype，达盖尔银版法，又称银版照相法，被公认为照相的起源，由达盖尔（Louis Daguerre）发明于1839年。在研磨过的银版表面形成碘化银的感光膜，于30分钟曝光之后，靠汞升华显影而呈阳图。当时，这种摄影方法的曝光时间大大地短于尼埃普斯（Joseph Nicéphore Nièpce）日光硬化的摄影方法。用这种方法拍摄出的照片具有影纹细腻、色调均匀、不易褪色、不能复制、影像左右相反等特点。——译者注

⑨ 同行的年轻人叫约翰·凡·涅斯特·打马字（Rev. John Van Nest Talmage），美国归正会教士，1847—1890年于厦门传教，创建和长期主理竹树脚基督堂，两任妻子、两个女儿均跟随他活跃于厦门。除传教外，打马字牧师大量译注《圣经》及相关书籍资料为厦门音白话字，以助推展教务之活动。其时在厦门亦有美国归正会、伦敦公会、英国长老会等差会，且合作从事厦门音白话字的发展工作。打马字博士一家和厦门有着难以割舍的情缘。他的第一任夫人艾比·打马字牧师娘(Abby Woodruff Talmage)新婚半年就随同丈夫，与罗啻夫妇同船来到厦门，在妇女中推广厦门音白话字，成为妇女工作的骨干，1862年2月长眠于厦门鼓浪屿崎仔尾传教士墓地。他的长女清洁·打马字（Katherine Talmage，人称"大姑娘"）、次女马利亚·打马字（Mary Elizabeth Talmage，"二姑娘"）出生在竹树脚，母亲逝世后被送回美国接受教育，1874年姐妹俩结伴重返厦门。大姑娘清洁在竹树脚创办第一所男童小学，为鼓浪屿养元小学前身；二姑娘马利亚在鼓浪屿创办田尾女学堂，即后来的毓德女子学校。博士的第二任夫人玛丽·打马字（Mary Eliza Talmage）于1865年伴随丈夫跨洋越海而来，在竹树脚创办女学。丈夫1892年于新泽西州逝世后，她又义无反顾地重返厦门，继续献身于妇女教育，直至1912年逝世，葬于崎仔尾传教士墓地，和艾比·打马字牧师娘做伴。打马字本人在厦门生活42年，他的4位女眷在厦门服务的时间加在一起长达180年。本书作者玛丽把打马字的姓氏Talmage异拼为Talmadge，自此之后的英文中，译者将其全部更正为Talmage。——译者注

⑩ 托马斯·狄维特·打马字（Thomas De Witt Talmage），是约翰·凡·涅斯特·打马字牧师的弟弟。19世纪末美国知名的牧师，曾担任过美国归正教会秘书，他牧养在纽约布鲁克林的归正教会中心教堂，影响力很大，许多信徒慕其名而来。打马字另有两个兄弟——詹姆斯（James）和戈因（Goyn）也是牧师，还有一个是成功的商人。他们的家族早年是随着新教教会从荷兰移民到北美洲来的。——译者注

第二章　厦门生活之一
Chapter 2　Life in Amoy（1）

［Communication Then and Now］

Think of the contrast—between that day of burdened and anxious waiting for months, for good or ill news; and this day when a few hours' time circles the globe, while day by day, if needed, communication can be made!

Soon after getting settled in their new home, a typhoon tore off the roof and let water pour in on them, which involved hurried moving to temporary shelter until a better building could be raised.

It appears as if father were somewhat of an architect, for among his papers there are drawings made to scale of the interior of the new home and also of the exterior as it would appear when completed, all in his own penmanship.

【通信今夕】

想想反差有多大吧：过去，人们心情沉重、心急火燎地煎熬数月，才能等来或好或坏的消息；而今天，几个小时就可以环绕地球一周，而且如果需要，每天都可以通信联络！

在新家安顿下来后不久，一场台风掀掉了屋顶，雨水兜头倾泻而下，他们急忙转移到临时避难所，等到更结实的房子建好。

父亲似乎有点建筑师天分，因为在他的文件中，有按比例绘制的新房子内部和外部完工后的效果图，都是他自己的笔迹。

时局：太平天国起义

哥哥查理是在1849年11月出生，我则出生在1851年9月。父母最初遭遇的一个体验便与太平天国起义有关。英国这边的军队指挥官被称为"中国的戈登"①。我记得有人指给我看楼梯垂直面上的弹孔，当时母亲怀抱着还是婴儿的查理就躲在那楼梯后面，免得给太平军和英军纷飞的流弹所伤。

有一发子弹刚好从她头顶上方的楼梯板穿过。我们常常看着另一个子弹，满心恐惧。那个子弹嵌在窗框里，也是那时候飞进来的。

还有一次，这是我自己记忆中的，我们周围的街道和码头上发生了骚乱。吃早饭时，父亲和母亲说话时语调严肃、焦虑，尽管我还是个小孩子，但也觉得心里很不安。枪声和尖叫声响起，后来我看到血淋淋的尸体从旁边漂过，母亲或者是父亲（他总是帮助、保护和照顾我）把我带走了，现在想来，他这样做再自然不过了，但我记得我很想回

Tide: Taiping Rebellion

My brother Charley came late in 1849, and my birthday was in September, '51. One of the first experiences met by my parents was in connection with the "Taiping Rebellion" in which "Chinese Gordon", as he was called, was British leader and here on the English side. I remember being shown a bullet hole in a stair rise behind which mother with her babe, Charley, in her arms was in hiding for protection against Chinese and British bullets, which flew all about the house.

One had come through this stair rise, just above her head. We often looked with awe at another, imbedded in a window casing, which came in at this same period.

Another time, within my own remembrance, there was a riot on the streets and wharfs about us. At breakfast father talked to mother in a serious, anxious tone, which—little child as I was—I felt troubled over. When shots and screams were heard, and later I saw bloody bodies floating by, I was taken away by mother or father (for he was always a helper, and guardian and caretaker), very naturally as we would think now, but I remember wanting to get back to the window, but was hindered!

A later time brought the scene of a quarrel in a boat at high tide, in which the boat upset; and when the tide went out, under the verandah windows was the body of one of the men. Charley was with me this time, and we were quickly led away; always there was the need of alertness in guarding the children from distressing or evil scenes. An insane man was chained between two logs, in a sail yard opposite our side windows, and left to cry and scream; and in a severe storm, the yard was flooded; and still he was there, causing tears of pity in parents and children. I often think of this scene, when reading of the demoniac among the stones in the Bible story.

I cannot follow events in sequence, or give assurance of their being really correct; and some of the maturer pictures had been made clear to me through having read their accounts in letters written by mother to her home circle. They were all included within seven full years, (for me) four of which must have held very dim, or no memories. Sam came late in '53, so there was a baby to love and watch over.

到窗口再看看，他却不让我看。

后来有个情景是，在涨潮的时候，船上发生了争吵，船翻了；当潮水退去后，在阳台窗户下面是某个船员的尸体。这次查理和我在一起，我们很快就被拉走离开窗前。家长总是需要时刻警惕，不让孩子看到痛苦或有害的场景。就在我们侧窗对面的船坞院子里，一个疯子被铁链锁在两根圆木之间，任由他在那里大哭大叫。后来，一场猛烈的暴风雨来了，院子被水淹没，那个人还在那里绑着，那惨状让父母和我们流下了同情的眼泪。当我读到《圣经》故事里被鬼附着的人的片段时，经常想起这一场景。

我无法按照先后顺序来叙述事件，也不能保证它们完全正确。在读过母亲写给她家人的信后，我才更全面地弄清一些情况。整整七年的生活都包含在内，但对我来说，其中的四年肯定很模糊，或者没有记忆。弟弟塞缪尔在1853年下半年出生，所以又多了一个婴儿要关爱和照顾。

【来自家乡的箱子】

就我的记忆力所及，箱子来自家乡的家人和朋友。开始时，印象很模糊。然后，似乎有什么非同寻常的事情发生了，所以朋友们常过来查看这些东西，并详尽地讨论一番。他们兴奋地大叫，互致问候。

后来，终于寄来了一个装着银版照片的箱子。母亲含着喜悦的泪水，用手轻抚照片，柔声地谈论着它们："这是妈妈"，"这是爸爸"。久久凝视着照片，看啊看，啊！多么美好，多么珍贵。箱子里还有给我们儿童读的书，及年龄大些后可以读的书。这些书也许是关于挪威海盗罗洛②的精彩好书（我们在厦门生活的日子里一直兴致勃勃地研读），或者是育儿歌谣什么的。有时还有衣服寄来，我们觉得很漂亮；寄给孩子们的衣服在我们看来就像关于罗洛的书里的男孩和女孩穿的衣服，看起来像美国孩子的样子，这是我们梦寐以求的。

父母高高兴兴地收到了干樱桃和葡萄干，对我们来说那只是坚硬的小石子和种

[Boxes from Home]

As long back as my memory can carry, boxes came from the homeland, from family and friends. Very dimly, at first, is the impress made. It seemed something very unusual had been happening, and great exclamations and greetings from friends who came in to see the things and talk them over.

Then, in time, there came a box with daguerreotypes, and tears of joy and brushing them away and talking softly over them—"this was ma" and "this pa"—O! So good and precious to look upon and pore over. And there were books for the children suitable for our tender age, and older ones as we grew older. Perhaps the wonderful Rollo books, which we pored over with thrills all the days we lived in Amoy, or "Songs for Little Children at Home". Clothes were sometimes sent, wonderful ones we thought, and when they were for the children, we thought they looked like the ones worn by the girls and boys in the Rollo books,—like American children—the height of our ambition.

Dried cherries and preserved currants—so happily received by our parents—were just little hard stones and seeds to us, which we did not like! Methods of sending to the Tropics, with long months of salt sea air surrounding them, had not developed, as in our day, and many things would not bear transportation. Only dried fruits could be counted on, as apples and cherries.

A trial was made of sending fresh apples, wrapped thoroughly in paper and in other ways protected. I can recall mother's and father's eagerness over them, as they unwrapped one, with bated breath, to see and taste the first fresh apple since they left "home", right from one of their choicest trees! But it was a solid mass of black decay! Then another one was unwrapped—just as spoiled! I remember mother saying, "Maybe there will be one good one, so we must try every one." But, alas, to no purpose! Then there was a bit of silence, while we children wondered.

A quilt was sent, quite early in the years, I think. Each one of many friends had made a block—with name and sentiment in the center—out of print material that mother would recognize as worn by friends in the homeland. The blocks were joined by white strips and on these, the names of all the brothers and father, and friends among her acquaintance, had been written, some with sen-

子，根本不喜欢！那个时候，向热带地区邮寄东西，还不像我们今天这样发达，好几个月在又咸又湿的空气中，很多东西都无法运输。只有苹果干和樱桃干等果干可以邮寄。

家人用新鲜苹果做了一回试验，把苹果用纸还有其他保护措施完全包好，邮寄过来。我能回忆起父母屏息解开一个苹果包装时的迫切心情，急着看看并品尝他们离开老家后的第一颗新鲜苹果，那可是家里最好的一棵苹果树上结的果子！但是，只有一团黑乎乎的腐果干结后的硬块。然后父母又解开一个苹果——还是烂的！我记得母亲说："也许总会剩下一个好果子，所以我们要把每一个都拆开。"但是，唉，白费功夫！接着是一阵沉默，而我们这些孩子却在纳闷怎么回事。

我记得是来厦门后头几年的时候，收到了寄来的一床百衲被。许多朋友每个人都用印花布料缝制一块儿，中间写着他们的名字和祝福，母亲能够认出来是谁谁谁在家乡时穿的衣服料子。一块又一块的布料用白色布条连缀在一起，上面写着她所有兄弟、父亲和熟识的朋友们的名字，有些人附带写上祝愿的话。就连老杰克、嬷嬷和家里其他黑人成员也请求给留一个"不起眼的角落"，让外祖母亲手写上他们的名字。

　　每当母亲生病，或哪怕是休息一天，她都会把被子展开盖在身上，然后把它拉到身边，带着爱意和思索，寻找一个又一个名字。她从中得到巨大的快乐，让我印象至深，因为她会大叫，"哦，这一块是妈妈的裙子"，"那是小莫利的婴儿装"，"这是伊莱扎·科布的名字"云云，直到把亲友们全部数一遍。通过念叨他们的名字，或她记得他们所穿衣服的料子，仿佛拉近了距离。这情景一直伴随着我，作为对母亲的快乐记忆之一。

【大桶黄油】

　　黄油是非常奢侈的东西，在厦门或那一带的任何地方都买不到，都是从亲爱的老家寄给母亲的。外祖母心甘情愿、吃苦受累，亲手制作黄油，以确保在制作过程中脱脂乳被完全分离，水分被完全挤干。她知道黄油要想储存并保持口味纯正、香甜，全靠这道工序，

timents attached. Even "old Jack" and "Granny" and other colored members of the family asked an "humble corner" written by grandmother's own hand.

　　Whenever mother was sick, or just resting a day off, she had her quilt spread over her, and would pull it about her, to find one and another name with loving reflections. The great delight it was to her made a deep impression on me, as she would exclaim, "Oh, here is a piece of ma's dress", "There is one of little Molly's baby dresses", "Here is Eliza Cobb's name", and so on through the whole number of dear ones, brought near by name, or dress material she remembered their wearing. It has always remained with me, as one of the happy memories of my mother.

[Hogsheads of Butter]

Butter was a great luxury, not to be procured in Amoy, or anywhere in that region, but it was sent to her from the loved home. Through the great labor of love of her mother, preparing the butter herself, lest all the buttermilk and water should not be absolutely extracted in the process of being made (knowing its being preserved, pure and sweet, depended on this work) it was made possible to send it to her in a well preserved condition.

And then the painstaking care of her father in packing it in small wooden kegs—previously prepared to receive the butter—sealed, and put into a hogshead covered with strong brine and headed up, completed its preparation.

This was continuously done for the beloved daughter during all her days, and after, until we all returned to this country, and by them shared with their friends. The coming of these hogsheads was another great event.

[Naughty MKs]

Sometimes there were naughty children who carried even in those tender years a sense of guilty consciences, but not heavy enough to cause confession of sins—only fear of exposure!

I was ringleader, I think, in throwing sand into some cups of rice in a basement window below us, but within our reach. Charley, Sam and I did this thing, and for all we knew or cared, in our hard hearts, it may be very likely that it caused some poor Chinese people to go hungry that day, since the poor always lived just on the borderland of starvation.

才有可能在保存完好的情况下邮寄到中国。

接下来，外祖父不辞辛苦地把黄油装进事先准备好的小木桶里，密封好，然后把这些小桶放进一个大桶里，装满浓盐水、桶口向上，完成了包装工作。

在母亲生前，外祖母和外祖父一直为心爱的女儿制作、邮寄黄油，他们的朋友帮忙分担一些工作。在母亲逝世后，直到我们全部回国之前也是如此。这些大桶黄油的到来是另一件大事。

【顽皮的熊孩子】

有时有些顽皮的孩子，处在稚嫩的年岁，即便良心上感到一丝负罪感，但还不足以严重到让他们忏悔自己的罪过，唯一害怕的是淘气被人发现！

楼下地下室窗子上有几碗米，刚好在我们够得着的距离内，我们往里面扔沙子，尽管我们心里都知道或者也很在意，它很可能会导致一些贫穷的中国人饿上一天，因为穷人总是挣扎在饥饿的边缘，但查理、塞缪尔和我还是这样干了。对于这件事，我想我是罪魁祸首。

我们经常听到船夫们粗声粗气、气呼呼的说话声，船就停在我家阳台长廊下面的码头附近。有时一看到我们，他们就骂我们"洋鬼子"，以及别的骂人话。

总而言之，我们这些孩子隐忍不住，要么制止他们争吵，要么为我们的冤屈报仇。所以，有一次我们把一大箱水兜头倒下，马上就听到他们连珠炮似的咒骂声，我们都吓坏了。

我们的父母没有听到叫骂声，否则我们更有理由吓得半死！我们过去经常坐我们的船四处兜风，但我记得那天下午，我恳求不要去码头坐船。我们这些犯错的孩子心惊胆战，紧紧抓住母亲的衣襟或父亲的手，四下张望，看看敌人是否会出现！但一切顺利，这些"少年犯"逃过一劫。

我们的房子

我们的房子建造在石墩和木墩上。房子的前部空间狭窄，但后面几个房间一直延伸至城市街道。它坐落于陆岬之上，两

We often heard rough, angry talk among boatmen, with boats lying close to the wharf below the verandah of our house, and sometimes, on seeing us, they called us names—"foreign devils", and other angry words.

Altogether, we children felt called upon to either rebuke their quarrels, or avenge our wrongs, so one time we poured a large carton of water down upon their heads, and were really quite frightened at the volley of curses poured out against us.

They were not overheard by our parents, or our cause of fright might have had more reason to exist! But I remember begging not to go down on the wharf to our boat (which we used often to go for a ride here and there) in that same afternoon, and it was with fear and trembling that we guilty children clung close to mother's skirts or father's hand, as we peered about to see if our enemy would appear! But all went well with the young sinners.

Our House

Our house was built on piers of stone and timber work. It was narrow across the front, but ran back several rooms deep to the city street. It was on a corner of land surrounded by tide water on two sides, with a wharf running by the side, the whole length back to the street. The back of the house faced the street, and contained quarters for the Chinese nurse and her family, and the servant.

Beginning from these quarters—toward the front and the waters were a hall and stairway and study. Then our parlor, or best room; next, a large storeroom with closets to the ceiling on three sides, and space for playroom too; beyond, two bedrooms and bathroom, following out to the narrow front of the house: all of these, aside from the "quarters", opened out on a verandah which embraced all of them back to the street or "quarters".

The veranda was shielded by sliding shutters, used to shelter from sun or storm, or drawn aside for breezes.

On the floor below these living rooms, on the street level, were the kitchen, and a bedroom for Jambi, the Malay cook. Toward the front was the dining room, and beyond, a room for meetings and gatherings with Chinese men or women, at different hours, for study or sociability with father and other missionaries.

There were bookcases here containing matter of interest to them.

Opening on our front water, through a heavily barred window high up from the floor, was a play

侧都被潮水包围着，一侧有个码头。房子一路延伸到街里，后面的部分临街，这里是中国保姆及其家人还有佣人的居室。

从后部的居室开始，朝前、朝海方向先是厅堂、楼梯和书房。然后是我们的起居室，或者叫会客室；接下来是一个大储藏室，三面墙都是壁橱，直通到天花板，还有游戏室的空间；再往远处，是两间卧室和一间浴室，一直延伸到房子狭窄的前部。有门通向阳台长廊，长廊在外部把所有房间连通起来，直通到后街或后部居室。

阳台长廊由滑动的百叶窗遮挡，用来挡住烈日或暴风雨，也可以拉到一边通风、透气。

我们起居室楼下是厨房和马来厨师占碑的卧室，和街道齐平。朝前走是饭厅，更远处是一个用来开会和聚会的房间，在不同时间段，华人在此向父亲和其他传教士学习，或进行社交活动。

这里有一些书柜，里面装着他们感兴趣的东西。

透过装着密密栏杆的落地窗，临着正前方海面的是一个游戏室兼杂物间。每当台风来临时，水位就会升高到离码头正面和侧面的窗口只差几英寸的地方。我们的记忆之一就是在一场大暴风雨过后，坐在餐厅深深的凸窗窗座上，伸手就能划水；而在通常的天气下，甚至是涨潮的时候，海水也不会淹没码头的窗户，而且来往的行人也够不着我们的窗户。我们坐在凸窗窗座里，从高处俯看着他们，显然，我们能听见他们彼此间谈论着我们。偶尔，那些从未见过外国人的人经过时，我们会听到他们说："瞧那蓝眼睛"，"看那粉红色的皮肤"，"他们的头发不像我们是黑色的，而是不同的颜色——红色、棕色等等"。

我们的家具自然是简单得很，有白色或红白相间的席子，许多藤编的椅子和长靠背椅，以及一些本地著名的雕刻品。

会客室里的家具更好一些，因为这里代表一个颇具影响力的大国——美国，接待来自不同国籍和不同社会阶层的客人。

会客室里的主要摆设有：最吸引眼球的是钢琴，中心镶嵌桃花心木的桌子，一些漂亮的中国小摆设，带格栅的大理石壁炉架，架子两侧是大约两英尺半或三英尺

room and catch all. At times of typhoons, the water would rise so high that it came within a few inches of the window-level on front and side of the wharf. One of our memories is of sitting on the deep window seats in the dining room and paddling in the water after one of these great storms, when, in usual weather, even at high tide, the water did not cover this part of the wharf, and men walking up and down could not reach up to our windows. Looking down upon them from our high perch, within our window seats, we could hear them talking to themselves about us, evidently. Occasionally, men who had never seen a foreigner passed and we heard, "See the blue eyes!" "Look at the pink skin!" or "Their hair is not black like ours, but different colors—red, brown, and so forth."

Our furniture was, naturally, very simple—white, or red and white check mattings, and a good deal of rattan in chairs and settees, with some of the noted carved pieces of native make.

The parlor, where guests of many nationalities and different ranks of society were entertained, as became a representative of one of the larger and most influential countries, had better furnishings.

The piano (first drawing card) and mahogany center table, some beautiful Chinese bric-a-brac, a marbleized mantelpiece with a grate, on both sides of which were Chinese vases about two and one-half or three feet high, were the chief articles. Tall stalks of rice paper flowers, much like double magnolia blossoms, pink and white, and leaves of cloth very naturally imitated, stood about four feet high in these vases. The vases I have here, you all know.

The carpet was of velvet, dark red with bright flowers over it. It seems to me it was bought in Boston and brought to Amoy with my parents, or it may, quite readily, have come from England with things brought by English or Scotch people.

It was much admired by our native and foreign friends: to the latter, "it looked like home"; to the former, very remarkable, but not nearly so fine as their own white mattings of soft, choice materials, woven into many figures—quite artistic indeed.

A singular incident about this carpet is that after coming to America, on the first visit we made to aunt Marcia Kitchell (Willis) to her home near Madison, N.J., we all exclaimed that the carpet was exactly like our own in Amoy, father confirmed it, too. The two sisters had shown the same taste, and chosen carpets alike; one bought in Boston in 1848, the other in New

高的中国花瓶。花瓶里插着几根高大的米纸花枝，大约有四英尺高，像两枝粉白相间的木兰花簇，用布仿造的叶子很自然。你们都看过的，花瓶现在就在我身边。

地毯是天鹅绒的，深红色，上面绣着鲜艳的花朵。在我看来，它是在波士顿买的，随我父母一起来到厦门。或者，我也愿意相信，它可能是英格兰人或苏格兰人从英格兰带来的东西。

地毯受到我们的中国和外国朋友一致赞赏：对后者来说，"它看起来像家一样"；对前者来说，这真了不起，但精致程度不如中国人自己的白色席子，席子材料柔软、上乘，还能编结出许多图案，事实上，颇具艺术性。

关于这块地毯还有一段奇异的插曲。我们到达美国后，第一次去拜访马西娅·基切尔（·威利斯）姨妈，她家在新泽西州麦迪逊镇附近。进门后，我们都惊叹她家地毯和我们在厦门的地毯一模一样，父亲也证实了这一点。姨妈和我母亲品位相同，挑选的地毯也一样；一件是1848年在波士顿买的，另一件是1858年或1859年在纽约买的——这两件地毯很可能最初都是从英国运来的。彼时的世界并非像我们这个时代这样迅速地变换，而且对真正价值的满足感不像今日这般短暂。

York City in 1858 or '59—both carpets were very likely sent from England originally. The world did not move quite so rapidly as in our days, and was content with good value for longer than now.

【注释】

① "中国的戈登"，即查尔斯·乔治·戈登（Charles George Gordon, 1833—1885），维多利亚时代的英国军官。由于在殖民时代异常活跃，被称为中国的戈登、喀土穆的戈登。他是一位管理能手，在领导常胜军时表现出一定战术技巧，但对宗教有异常的癖好，自信宗教具有神奇的力量，可以影响异民族。1852年，戈登从军校毕业，进入皇家工兵部队，军衔少尉，派到威尔士潘布卢克（Pembroke）修建海港设施。1854年，戈登自告奋勇加入英国远征军到克里米亚参战。1860年，第二次鸦片战争爆发，他志愿到了中国，并在9月抵达天津。他没赶上对大沽炮台的攻击，不过赶上占领北京的行动。他在中国北方一直待到1862年4月，直到太平天国开始在上海威胁到欧洲人为止。形势所迫，上海成立了一支由欧洲人和清军组成的义勇军来防御太平军。这支军队由美国人华尔（Frederick Townsend Ward）指挥。华尔在对慈溪的攻击时阵亡。1863年3月，在李鸿章的赏识和推荐下，戈登在松江接任了指挥，他手拿小藤条严加训练部队，并屡屡凶狠出击，于是部队得到一个用来鼓励但夸张的称号——常胜军。戈登重整了军队并成功支援常熟，很快得到士兵们的尊敬。11月，苏州被戈登和清军（淮军）合力攻下，郜云官等降将被清军所杀。戈登因苏州杀降与李鸿章产生嫌隙。1864年5月，太平军在天京（今南京）外围的最后一个堡垒常州失陷，常胜军的声望也达到最高峰。太平天国运动被中外势力联合绞杀，战争结束。清朝同治皇帝授予戈登清军最高军阶——提督的称号；另外，英国也晋升他为中校并封他为（爵位等级最低的）巴思爵士。此后，戈登转战非洲苏丹和中东等地。由于他笃信宗教，被一些人视为基督战士和英雄，20世纪的现代英国仍有城市和组织以不同形式对他表示纪念。——译者注

② 罗洛（Rollo, 860?—931?），亦称罗尔夫（Hrólf），古斯堪的纳维亚海盗首领，维京海盗的传奇英雄之一，诺曼底公国的第一位公爵，查理大帝的祖先。在896—911年这15年间里，他率队沿着法兰克北部海岸线劫掠，到达

塞纳河流域。由于罗洛身材太过高大不能骑马（没有马匹能够载得动他），到任何地方去都得步行，所以人们就冠以"步行者罗洛"之称。911 年，罗洛进军塞纳河并围攻巴黎，虽然最后打不下巴黎撤退了，但是却沿海岸线占领了大量的殖民地并定居下来。最后迫使法王查理三世在 911 年与其签订了《圣·克莱尔 - 苏尔 - 埃普特条约》，封他为公爵，将塞纳河口一带地方划归他统治，他成为基督教徒并被查理三世封臣，以后这里有大批维京人前来定居，这片土地被北欧海盗蚕食，逐渐形成诺曼底公爵领。——译者注

第三章　厦门生活之二

Chapter 3　Life in Amoy (2)

【7月4日 ① 的国庆聚会】

在我们起居室楼上是一个开放的阳台，四周用漂亮的砖墙围着，晚上我们经常去那里乘凉。我记得在那里举办过一次著名的国庆聚会。

客人包括一位美国领事，以及几位英国和荷兰领事；英格兰、苏格兰及美国传教士；几位英格兰和苏格兰茶商以及他们的妻子——英格兰的包义德 ② 夫妇、苏格兰的赛姆夫妇，他们都是父母的好朋友。这几家交往频繁，关系融洽。还有来自美国的一支小舰队"勇士"号的军官、英国皇家海军舰艇的军官，以及其他一众人。

我们唱着美国歌曲《致敬哥伦比亚》③、

[4th of July Party]

Above our living floor was an open verandah, well railed in fancy brick work wall, where we often went for cool breezes in the evenings. I remember a famous Fourth of July party held up there.

The guests were the American Consul, and the British and Dutch Consuls. There were English and Scotch missionaries, and the American ones, and several English and Scotch tea merchants, and their wives, who were mother's and father's warm friends,—Mr. and Mrs. Boyd of England, and Mr. and Mrs. Syme of Scotland, who formed a very congenial social group. There were officers from our own small fleet of "Men of War", as they were called in those days, and British officers of "H.M.S.'s", more numerous.

We sang National Airs—"Hail

Columbia", "Yankee Doodle", and "God Save The King" to our own tune of "America". I do not recall "The Star Spangled Banner", and hardly think that had drifted so far from America, or perhaps it was too near facts to be an acceptable song between Britons and Americans! There were wonderful fireworks in the Sail Yard, just opposite us (where the poor insane man had been chained). Father was ingenious in planning some of them, and Chinese skill carried out. China is the home of fireworks, as we know. One that father planned was a large illumination of "E Pluribus Unum". I should say the letters were a foot long or more. Another was a rowboat full of people, who pulled oars in unison as it ran over the ground. I do not vouch this to be a fact, but it certainly is the impression left on my mind. There was a high fountain of sparks such as we sometimes see yet. Pleasant banter between English, Scotch and Americans occupied some of the time, between these friends up there on the roof of our home.

English Friends & the Crimean War

Another scene comes to mind with English friends.

《扬基歌》④ 和《天佑吾王》⑤。我不记得是否唱过《星条旗之歌》⑥，也不认为它已经漂洋过海从美国来到中国，或许这首歌太接近现实，无法让英美两国人民共同接受。美妙的烟花就在我们对面的船坞院子（那可怜的疯子被锁在那里）燃放。父亲构思了其中一些创意烟花，中国工匠付诸实施。众所周知，中国是烟花的故乡。父亲的创意之一是一个大烟花空中炸开后，映出"合众为一"⑦字样。我想这些字母的大小每个都有一英尺以上。另一个图案是一艘载满人的小船，众人齐声划桨划过搁浅的沙滩。我不保证与事实相符，但这肯定是我脑海中留下的印象。还有一个烟花是我们有时看到的那种，烟火像喷泉一样高高地向上喷涌。聚会的一部分时光消磨在朋友们之间愉快的谈笑逗趣中，就在我们家屋顶上，有英格兰人、苏格兰人和美国人。

英国朋友及克里米亚战争 ⑧

另一幅浮现在脑海中的场景是有关英国朋友的。父母坐在楼下的阳台上，那是我们家最凉爽、大家最经常去的地方，有几个英格兰商人来访。

他们给我们带来一幅彩色地图，标注着塞瓦斯托波尔战役的走势。在1854—1856年 [9] 的克里米亚战争中，塞瓦斯托波尔是军事行动的焦点。现在，硝烟散去了一些时日，战争图辗转到了厦门，尽管战争的记忆在他们的脑海中依然鲜活如新。

这些英国朋友极度兴奋，从表现来判断，他们大概参加过这场战役。我记得，当他们指着这一处或那一处战场，描述他们与敌人相遇的情形时，兴奋得大叫并热烈地谈论着。我当时一定很小，因为在地图上看到散布各处的红线和红色的小人时，我想这些一定是战场喋血的写照！

与我们的英国朋友另一次的接触很有趣，1930年秋天，他们给我哥哥查理一个1851年合订本的《伦敦新闻画报》，里面有第一届美洲杯帆船赛 [10] 的记录，比赛在英国水域进行，这个比赛被引进到这个国家，此后一直延续下去。书中有第一届赛事中划船的照片，还有冠军奖杯的照片。也是这次见面，一个年轻人给了

Father and mother were seated on the lower verandah, which we used oftenest as the coolest spot in our house, and some English merchants were calling.

They brought a colored map and illustrations of the battle of Sebastopol, which had been fought in the Crimean War of 1854-1856. Now, somewhat later, though fresh in their minds, these had found their way into Amoy.

Probably the Englishmen had been in the battle, judging from the intense excitement they showed, as I recall, as they pointed out this spot or that, and described encounters, with exclamations and enthusiastic conversation between them all. I must have been very young, for looking at the red lines here and there and red figures of men, I thought these must be pictures of bloodshed in the battle!

Another touch of interest with our British friends, especially this fall of 1930, was the presenting to my brother Charley of a bound volume of *Illustrated London News* for 1851, containing the account of the first race for the America's cup, run in British waters, in which the cup was brought to this country—and has remained here ever since. There are pictures of the boats in that first race, and of the Cup won. At the same time, one of the young men also gave me a paper weight in which the picture of Prince Albert was encased. He was still living at that time, and he and Queen Victoria appeared to be much beloved by the English colony in Amoy; and this glass paper weight with his picture, was given to me as something of special value.

[Gulangyu's First Piano]

The young tea merchants often called at our home, and enjoyed mother's singing and playing on the piano for them. She was the only one who possessed a piano, of the entire foreign colony. It is on record that an Englishman asked father's permission, most courteously, if he might present her with one. There were a few "melodeons", but no other piano!

These young men brought pieces of music for her to play or sing for them—just new then "Lily Dale", "Who'll Buy a Calla Herring from a Scotchman", and "Blue Bells of Scotland", "Auld Lang Syne", " "Sweet Afton", "Annie Laurie", and others.

She often sang to other groups,—or to her own family, the old darkey songs, "Old Virginny", "Rosa Lee", "Up and Down thee Swanee River", "Old Kentucky

我一个镇纸，里面装着阿尔伯特亲王的画像。当时他还活着，他和维多利亚女王似乎很受在厦门的英国人士爱戴。这张带着他照片的玻璃镇纸作为礼物，有着特殊的价值。

【鼓浪屿的第一架钢琴】

年轻的茶商们经常来我家做客，他们很喜欢母亲的歌声和钢琴演奏。母亲是鼓浪屿上唯一一个拥有钢琴的人。据记载，有个英格兰人极有礼貌地询问父亲，可否允许他送给母亲一架钢琴。岛上有几台小型簧风琴，但没有其他的钢琴。

这些年轻人给她带来了一些乐谱，让她演奏或演唱给他们听，有当时的新歌《百合谷》《谁会从苏格兰人那里买一只马蹄鲱鱼》《苏格兰的蓝铃花》《友谊地久天长》《甜蜜的阿夫顿》《安妮·劳里》[11]等。

她也经常为其他群体或是自己的家人唱古老的黑人歌曲，如《老弗吉尼》[12]《罗莎·李》《走遍斯旺尼河》《肯塔基老家》，还有《夏日的最后一朵玫瑰》[13]，还有许多其他的曲子。这些曲子我一直铭记在心，大家似乎都很熟悉，所以当我们到达美国后，这些曲子就变成了钢琴旁的"合唱会"。在厦门，我们这些孩子经常和母亲一起唱歌，唱我们孩子能粗浅理解的歌曲，还有她最初教我们的圣歌歌词。中国妇女似乎被这能发出如此悦耳声音的乐器和歌声迷住了，男人们也很好奇，所以时不时地来我们家拜访。

与军人交往：佩里准将访问厦门

英国军舰经常停泊在港口，父母熟悉的军官或由老友陪着的新军官就会来访。有一个温馨的故事，发生在我还不记事的时候，讲的是一个军官在我家病得很重，母亲精心照料他，为他准备开胃的食物，等等。军官离开后，从伦敦给母亲寄来一条漂亮的、长长的纯金表链和一封诚挚的感谢信，这两件东西现在都在我的手里。

我们美国的海军军官也同样来我家做客。佩里准将在中国和日本海域执行任务

Home". Also the "Last Rose of Summer", and many others whose tunes I have carried always, and which seemed old familiar ones, when transferred to the "sings" around the piano after we reached America. We children often sang with her, songs within our childish comprehension, and hymns whose words she taught us first. The Chinese women seemed spellbound at the instrument, as well as the voice, producing such sweet sounds. Men, too, wondered, as they came among us for calls now and then.

Association with Navy Officers: Commodore Perry Visited Amoy

Ｂritish warships often anchored in the harbor, when their officers who were acquainted, or new ones who accompanied them called on us. A pleasant story, before my days of remembering, is of an officer's becoming very ill at our home, and of mother's nursing him, and preparing appetizing food for him, and so forth. When he left, he sent to her from London a beautiful long watch chain of gold, and a very grateful letter of appreciation, both of which are in my possession now.

Our own Navy officers came to us in the same way. Commodore Perry visited us more than once, while on duty in Chinese and Japanese waters. The last time, I must have been developing my interest in sewing, for, reading between the lines, mother must have been telling him that I could sew (at six years of age), and he made a great pet of me, bringing out a white silk handkerchief, and saying pathetically he wished he could have it marked so it would not get lost. I at once offered to embroider his name on it, which deed was profusely and gratefully accepted.

Mother produced some pink sewing silk and marked a "P" in a corner, and I embroidered it—beautifully, in my own estimation, I remember! I was greatly praised for it by the Commodore, with expressions of gratefulness that now it would never be lost; and I can still feel the swell of my little heart over the good deed. My sewing skill did not lessen in my own estimation.

[Original Sin: Lying]

Mother once set me to hemming a handkerchief, and I reasoned if I could hem finely enough, the stitches would not show at all, so why not cut the task short by telling my mother I had finished it? When she remonstrated with me with, "Why! my child, you have not hemmed it at all", I looked right into her face,

时，不止一次拜访过我们。最后一次，我那时一定是对缝纫产生了兴趣，因为话里话外，母亲一直在和他说我在六岁的年纪就会针线活。他很宠我，拿出一条白色真丝手帕，怜惜地说他希望能给它做个标记，这样就不会弄丢了。我立刻表示愿意在上面绣上他的名字，对于此举，他赞不绝口，欣然接受。

母亲做了一些粉红色的缝纫丝线，在角落里标出一个字母"P"，我把它绣了出来——我记得绣得很漂亮，自我感觉良好！我受到了准将的高度赞扬，他感激地说，此后再也不会把它弄丢了。我现在还能感觉到当时我的小心脏因为这桩好事而砰砰地跳。我的缝纫技术还是货真价实的！

【原罪：小孩儿撒谎】

有一次，母亲让我给手绢缝褶边，我推断，如果我能缝得够细，针脚就根本看不出来，那么，为什么不干脆告诉母亲我已经缝好了呢？当她发现后责备我说："为什么？我的孩子，你根本就没缝。"我恬然无知地看着她的脸，说我已经缝好了，只是缝得太细了，她看不见。我又被责备一遍，但顽固地坚持说已经缝过了。我仍然记得父母流露出惊恐的神色，因为这么厚颜无耻的谎言竟是从一个稚气未脱的孩子嘴里说出来的！

然后怀着极度沉痛的心情，我被带进书房，独自一人去反思我的罪过。至于未来的父母对犯了错的孩子说的灰心丧气之类的话，我不记得他们对我说过，也不记得我那时是怎么想的。但我没有被打屁股，这我记得很清楚。过了一会儿，母亲来了；（这可能是最灵验的疗法，）她伤心地看着我的眼睛，我用胳膊搂住她的脖子，她也搂着我，我哭了，她亲了亲我，于是我们和好了。但我再也不像以前那样轻易地、不计后果地撒谎了！

依照当时的神学理论，我设想父母自言自语地说："这是'原罪论'的一个可怕例子和确证。"因它竟然在他们如此精心培育、教导和为之祈祷的孩子身上显现出来！

with all the assurance of ignorance, and said, I had finished it, only it was done with such small stitches she could not see them. I was remonstrated with again, and stoutly maintained that it was sewed; and still I remember the look of horror which passed between my parents over such a brazen lie, coming out of nearly baby lips!

And then with what sorrow I was led into the study and left there alone to think over my sin.—For the disheartening of future parents with little sinners, I do not remember anything that was said to me, or what I thought about. I was not spanked—that I know—and after a while mother came; (and this probably was the most efficacious treatment) and looked very sadly into my eyes, and I threw my arms about her neck, and she me, and I cried and she kissed me, and we made up. But I never told lies again as easily or with as little care for consequences!

I suppose my parents said to themselves, out of the Theology of those days: "This is a terrible example of, and confirmation of the 'Doctrine of Original Sin'", that it should reveal itself in a child of theirs, so carefully nurtured and taught and prayed over!

Heretics?

And, just then, two here-
tics may have been born
who dared to doubt the authority
of Great Councils, met in convoca-
tions; for among father's papers are
copies of letters of protest sent to
the Foreign Missions Commission
of the Dutch Reformed Church,
against the Walls of Sectarianism,
all built on the Authority of Councils as to what were true creeds
and doctrines to be obeyed. He was
pleading for unity in work among
Missions. This happened long,
long years ago, before this day of
Grace—with the subject still protested and unsettled!

Patience and Loving Care

One lesson was always im-
pressed upon us children
from our earliest days; "Thou, God,
seest me.", and as our conception
of God was of One who loves us,
this little verse accompanied by this
impression, I do most heartily in-
dorse as a strong preventative to all
impure thoughts and wrong-hearted
deeds—the stated lie to the contrary
notwithstanding—so keeping the
channel open to hearing "Do unto

异端邪说?

就在那个时候，父亲和打马字牧师可
能发出了不同的声音。他们在主教区会议中
意见一致，大胆质疑总会的权威，因为在父
亲的文件中，有几份寄给美国荷兰归正教会
海外差传委员会的抗议信，反对宗派主义的
门户之见。宗派主义在关于什么是信徒应该
遵守的真信条和真教义问题上，一切建立在
总会的权威基础上。他请求各差会在工作中
团结一致。这件事发生在很久很久以前，这
个话题时至今日依然遭到反对和怀疑。⑭

耐心与呵护

我们从孩提时起，就一直铭记"耶和
华为看顾人的神"这条训导。"神爱世人"
是我们对上帝的理解，因此这一行短小精
悍的诗文及其所产生的影响，我由衷地赞
同，认为它能有力地预防一切不纯洁的思
想和不道德的行为，前文提到的撒谎之事
是个反例，所以要敞开心扉聆听"己所不
欲，勿施于人"和"彼此相爱"的教诲。

我希冀把我这次对父母内心与用意的洞察记录下来，记录下他们对孩子始终如一、充满爱意的呵护和关怀。

我回想起母亲有一次对我表现出有忍耐的失望。在储藏室里有一个大篮子，它的盖子分两半，从中间向两头翻开。如果把篮子侧放时，盖子就成了门。我想到个主意，在这里面玩过家家，而且很快就玩疯了，疯上了天。我会经常爬进爬出我的房子，为我孩子的家提供食物，或假装戴上帽子去拜访朋友。直到……天啊！母亲的声音传来时，我所有的生活计划都被打断了。她叫喊道："哦！玛丽！看看你都做了些什么！你漂亮的蓝裙子被撕成了碎片！"但我却没听到一句责骂声。我裙子上面的图案是白色棕榈叶。篮子里的编织条勾住我的裙子，留下无数个"蝙蝠耳朵"一样的洞。

但母亲的话到此为止，没有更多可轻可重、可深可浅的贬损话，不过我那件漂亮的蓝白相间的连衣裙留不住了。父亲走进现场，脸上流露出对母亲赞同、对我责备的神情。

others—" and "Love one another." This little insight into the heart and purpose of my parents I wish to leave on record of the loving care and thought always faithfully and lovingly given to their children.

I recall the patient despair of my mother shown toward me at one time. There was a large basket in the store-room with two half lids opening and shutting from the center to the ends of it, and when laid on its side, produced doors of the lids. I conceived the idea of playing house in this, and was soon soaring up in the clouds. I had occasion to crawl in and out of my house very often, to provide for my family of children, or to call on friends after making motions of putting on my bonnet. When, Lo! All my schemes of life were cut short, as mother's voice called, "O! Pussy! See what you have done! Your pretty blue dress (covered with a pattern of little white palm leaves) all torn to pieces!" And I do not catch the echo of a cross word said! The splints in the basket had caught the dress, and made innumerable "bats' ears"!

But the words said were enough to stop future depreciations into unknown consequences, and my pretty blue and white dress disappeared. Father came in on the scene with looks of sympathy for mother and reproof for me.

[Candy Stories]

Out of this same store room, all lined with closets and cupboards, comes a vision of standing in front of mother with my brothers, Charley and Sammy, and baby Marcia, to receive in our hands delightful little pink and white peppermint candies, taken from a large mouthed glass bottle, which we eagerly watched her lift down from O! so high up, we thought—I wonder why?—and put her hand into to get for us. I think these candies came in the boxes from home, kept replenished "for the children".

Sweets were dealt out to us from another source which comes into mind with this scene. There was a Chinese friend who evidently came into our lives occasionally when returning to Amoy. He was welcomed warmly by all of us, I remember, and he always brought us a cake of sugar preparation which looked as large as a cheese ten inches in diameter, I should say, to our childish eyes; but judging from the way sizes which are immense in children's eyes, dwindle down as the years increase, may have been about three inches in diameter—just big enough to be chipped off a number

【糖果故事】

就在同一间储藏室，它四边排立着高高的壁柜和食橱，一幅场景闪现在眼前：我与哥哥查理、弟弟萨米⑮，还有仍是婴儿的马西娅一起站在母亲面前，伸手接着可爱的粉红色和白色的小薄荷糖果。糖果是从一个大嘴玻璃瓶里拿出来的，我们眼巴巴地看着她把瓶子从我们认为很高的地方托举下来，把手伸进去给我们拿糖。我想不明白，瓶子为什么放这么高？我想这些糖果装在盒子里，从老家寄来，是为孩子们不断备足的。

从这个场景联想到给我们分发来自另一个渠道的甜食的情形。有一个中国朋友，他回到厦门时偶尔会来拜访我们。我记得他受到我们大家的热烈欢迎，他总是给我们带一块糖做的蛋糕，我得说，在我们孩童眼里，蛋糕看起来足有直径十英寸的奶酪那么大；但是，孩子们眼睛里的尺寸巨大，随着年龄的增长，会逐渐缩小，这样看来，蛋糕的直径可能三英寸左右——大小仅够切几刀，一天又一天，直到美食被吃光。

我又想起了一个糖果故事。时不时有中国货郎或者小贩从街上走进我们房子的大厅，我们被喊下楼看他们的货物。一般他们肩上的扁担一端挑着长方柜，另一端要么是一个晃荡的炭盆，要么是另一个长方柜，具体根据卖的货物而定。那个卖糖果的小贩有热乎的软糖，或者在炭火上融化，他再用吹玻璃的方法吹出人和物来，有些造型质朴，有些像棒棒糖，父亲母亲会给我们买。我记得在我们眼前吹出过一只公鸡，尾巴上插着一截苇秆，这样就可以让它打鸣啼叫，我们高兴得不得了。另一个摊贩会展示漂亮的丝绸或刺绣品，以及今天我们在他们精致的作品中依旧还能见到的各种色调精美的丝织物。这些丝织物在我们的衣橱里或市场上也能看到。

有这么多的人口，饮食是随随便便就能兴旺起来的生意，这些街头小贩做得红红火火：卖一碗米饭，或一点儿蔬菜，或鼎边趖及其他简单的食物。人们花不了几毛钱，

of times for a delicious treat, day by day until all was eaten.

Another candy story comes to mind. Chinese peddlers, or venders, carrying cabinets hung on one end of a pole placed across the shoulders, and on the other end, either a brazier of charcoal swung, or another cabinet, according to the articles for sale, came now and then into the hall from the street, and we were called downstairs to see their wares. The candy man had fondant keeping hot, or melted over the fire, and he would blow figures after glass blowers' methods, some very ingenious, some like lollipops; and father or mother would buy them for us. I remember a rooster which was blown before our eyes, which had a bit of reed in its tail, so arranged as to cause a crowing—to our great delight. Another vender would show beautiful pieces of silk, or of embroidery, and skeins of silks of all the delicate shades which we recognize in their fine work in this day, which has found its way into our wardrobes or markets.

Food was such a casual article with multitudes of the people that a brisk trade was carried on by these street venders, who sold a bowl of rice, or a bit of vegetable, or boiled dough, and other simple edibles, for a few cash, gladly bought by many to soothe the gnawings of hunger;

or there would be better food and treats for the well-to-do.

[The Barber]

The barber had his following, too. He carried his shaving implements around from door to door, and was hailed in passing, or solicited a job of shaving heads back to the place where the queue began, in those old days where queues were commanded, to show submission from the Chinese to the Manchurian Empire. Besides shaving heads, the barber massaged the eyeballs—and another illustration that "there is nothing new under the sun. He also cleansed the ears before completing his job.

We children liked to slip down to the kitchen to visit old Jambi, though were soon brought back to our own floor by our old boa, or nurse. Jambi was a Malay, and had a smile for us or a bit of sweets. He specially petted Sammy and Mousie, the younger ones. The latter was still learning to talk readily, and mixed all three languages: our own, the Chinese, and Malay tongue, in a single sentence. Even when we first arrived here, at four years of age she chattered often in the triple languages combined. However, this was soon dropped, having been separated three or more months from their influence, it was forgotten.

高兴地买来，慰藉一下辘辘饥肠的折磨；还有给有钱人准备的更好的美味佳肴。

【剃头匠】

剃头匠也有追随者。他用担挑着剃头工具挨家挨户地走街串巷，路过时有人把他叫住剃头，即把头发削剪到原本留发蓄辫的地方。在旧时，削发垂辫是强制的，是汉人向大清帝国屈服的标志。除了剃头，剃头匠还给人滚眼 ⑯，这是"世界之大无奇不有"的又一例证。他还给顾客掏耳朵，这样才算齐活儿。

我们这些孩子喜欢溜到厨房去看老占碑，不过很快就被我们的老保姆带回我们自己的楼层。占碑是一个马来人，对我们笑呵呵的，还给糖吃。他特别宠爱萨米和最小的莫西 ⑰。莫西刚刚学着说话，一句话里会夹杂三种语言：英语、汉语和马来语。甚至当我们刚到这儿的时候，她四岁时就经常用三种语言夹杂着说话。然而，由于分开三个月或更长时间，这种影响很快就消失了，也就忘记了。

【每日菜单】

占碑以前每天都到楼上和母亲商量当天的菜单，尽管菜单很简单。我不记得母亲会去厨房监督做饭，除了一次做番石榴果冻。我也跟着去了，看着占碑的大手把果汁从布里挤出来，鲜红的果冻被放进罐子里，用白纸盖上（那时还没有漂亮的盖子）。

我们惯常是吃米饭的，而且总是加红糖一起吃，这美味我从来没有吃够过，直到今天，还是喜欢它俩的组合。有咖喱螃蟹和咖喱鱼，鸡、羊、红薯，特别美食是汽船运来的一些白土豆。在我吃来，它们也很差劲，又苦涩又皱巴。山药成了我们的常备食物。除了热乎乎的英国松饼外，我想不起桌上有什么热的或是冷的面包或饼干；但我确定有面包和红糖。在适当的时机和场合，还有布丁和蛋糕，我们很喜欢用华夫烤炉做的蛋糕，一边还能数着烤模上面的格子。当然，还有很多应季水果。这些东西在我脑海里印象深刻，尽管我毫

[Daily Menu]

Jambi used to come upstairs daily to consult with mother about the day's menu—very simple though it was. I do not remember mother's going to the kitchen to supervise any cooking, except once to make guava jelly. I tagged along too, and have a vision of the juice being squeezed through a cloth by Jambi's big hands, and of the rich red jelly being put into jars which were covered with white paper (no fine lids in those days!).

Our food was rice, continually, and always eaten with brown sugar, whose good taste I have never lost and enjoy the combination to this day. There were crabs and fish, with curry, and chicken, and lamb, and sweet potatoes, and as a great treat, a few white potatoes which had been brought in by some steamer; and very poor and bitter and puckery they were, too, to my taste. Yams were our standbys instead. I have no recollections about bread or biscuit, hot or cold, except hot English muffins, on the table; but bread and brown sugar was served to us, I do know. There were puddings and cake in their proper time and place—cake made in waffle irons was our delight, as we counted the window panes in them—and of course, much fruit in their season. These articles stand out in my mind, though I have no doubt there were others—perhaps some not good for little children.

One more service from Jambi looms up before me. We had two kittens—white to begin with—Tommy and Tatty, and very precious. Every day he brought up to our verandah a dish of boiled rice with little fishes mixed together, for their food (the tiny fish not more than an inch long).

Our old Boa was very faithful and full of affection for us, always alert to guard us and do mother's bidding. She had a young woman daughter who lived in the back quarters with her, and assisted her mother with the four of us at times. A son of hers also, who carved nuts in wonderful designs, or figures and animals, for his living, seemed to be often there; and I was fascinated in watching him use the tiny, sharp knives or chisels and other very diminutive tools. I even asked him to let me try to do it, but he shook his head very positively! I think I must have had some of the assurance of present day Young America!

不怀疑还有其他的——也许有些对小孩子健康不好的东西。

我又想起占碑的另一项任务。我们有两只小猫——汤米和泰缇，它们一出生是白色的，非常珍贵。占碑每天都在我们阳台放上一盘掺了小鱼（小鱼不超过一英寸长）的米饭，作为猫食。

我们的老保姆非常忠诚，对我们充满了爱，总是警惕地守护着我们，听从母亲的吩咐。她有一个年轻的女儿，和她一起住在后面的房子里，她女儿有时帮助她照顾我们四个孩子。她还有一个儿子，以雕刻核桃为生，或是雕精美图案，或是雕人物和动物。他似乎经常待在那里。我很着迷地看着他用锋利的小刀、凿子和其他小工具雕刻。我甚至要求他让我试一试，但他非常肯定地摇了摇头。我想我一定拥有今天新兴美国的某种自信！

【注释】

① 7月4日，美国国庆日，是美国的主要法定节日之一，以纪念1776年7月4日大陆会议在费城正式通过《独立宣言》。——译者注

② 包义德（T. D. Boyd），英国人，1878年厦门共济会组合早期成员。厦门鼓浪屿曾经有3个英国共济会秘堂。——译者注

③《致敬哥伦比亚》，也称《美国万岁》，一首美国爱国歌曲。在1931年胡佛（Herbert Hoover）总统宣布《星条旗》为美国国歌前约100年时间里，两者一直竞争当国歌。——译者注

④《扬基歌》，美国内战时流行的一支歌曲，也被称为美国的准国歌，被认为是美国最流行的歌曲之一。"扬基"意为北方佬，指内战期间的北方（联邦）军队的士兵。——译者注

⑤《天佑吾王》，英国国歌。——译者注

⑥《星条旗之歌》，又作《星光灿烂的旗帜》，美国国歌，美国律师弗朗西斯·斯科特·基（Francis Scott Key）作词，配上英国作曲家约翰·斯塔福德·史密斯（John Stafford Smith）的乐曲而成。——译者注

⑦ "合众为一"，E Pluribus Unum，拉丁语，尤指类似于美国的由诸州联合组成的全国政府，1956年前曾作为美国国训，现今作为铭文用于美国国玺和部分钱币上。——译者注

⑧ 克里米亚战争，又名克里木战争、东方战争、第九次俄土战争。在1853年10月20日因争夺巴尔干半岛的控制权而在欧洲大陆爆发的一场战争，是拿破仑帝国崩溃以后规模最大的一次国际战争，奥斯曼帝国、英国、法国、撒丁王国等先后向俄罗斯帝国宣战。——译者注

⑨ 原文此处把克里米亚战争的时间说成1854—1856年，并不完全正确。克里米亚战争的过程分为几个阶段：最初是1853年11月俄土两国参加的锡诺普海战（Sinop Naval），然后是1854年1月英法参战，随后战争扩大，联军形成，还有黑海之外其他战场同时开战。作者提及的1854—1856年大概说的是英法参战后的时间段。——译者注

⑩ 美洲杯帆船赛是帆船赛中影响最大、声望最高的赛事，与奥运会、世界杯足球赛、一级方程式赛车并称"世界范围内影响最大的四项传统体育赛事"。——译者注

⑪《安妮·劳瑞》，这首歌的词是18世纪苏格兰作家威廉·道格拉斯（William Douglas）写给他的意中人的，尽管他一片痴情，可安妮并没有成为他的妻子。歌词在流传中曾多次被人改动，最后传到一位业余作曲家斯考特夫人（Lady John Scott, 1810—1900）手中，她改定了歌词并谱了曲，1838年首次发表时并没有署名，当时斯考特夫人才28岁，还是一个默无名声的女子。1853—1856年克里米亚战争期间，这首歌曲曾在军队中广为流传。——译者注

⑫ 作者玛丽写的是19世纪50年代的事，但是《老弗吉尼》这首歌却是在1878年谱写的，因此她晚年记忆并不准确。"Old Virginny"全名叫"Carry me Back to Old Virginny"（《把我带回弗吉尼故乡》），是詹姆斯·布兰德（James A. Bland, 1854—1911）创作的其最优秀的作品。作为一个黑人作曲家，他一生创作了约700首歌曲，并于1879年参加了一个由真正黑人组成的黑艺人表演团，到大西洋沿岸诸城进行演出，后又去苏格兰跟英格兰巡回演出，取得了极大的成功。他在英国待了近20年后回国。——译者注

⑬ 《夏日的最后一朵玫瑰》，是一首古老的爱尔兰民歌，是世界上广为流传的爱尔兰抒情歌曲。它原来的曲名叫作《年轻人的梦》（"Castle Hyde"），后来一个叫米利金（R. A. Millikin）的人给它重新填词，改名为《布拉尼的小树林》（"The Grooves of Blarney"）。到了19世纪，爱尔兰的著名诗人托马斯·摩尔（Thomas Moore）对它发生兴趣，可是他对前面那两种词都不满意，于是又重新为它填了词，改名为《夏日的最后一朵玫瑰》。歌词内容略带伤感，借夏天最后一朵玫瑰来比喻爱情和青春即将凋谢，抒发对美好事物逝去的依恋心情。——译者注

⑭ 此处的纷争指的是闽南地区中国教会自立过程中罗啻、打马字等同美国归正教会总会意见分歧，坚持教派联合、本地教会自立一事。
　　早在1856年，罗啻、打马字等美归正会宣教士，就看到了中国人自主办教会的必要性，因为只有华人担负起牧养教会的重任，才能消除文化上的隔阂，更好地传播福音。他们组建了筹委会，并邀请英国长老会的杜嘉德（Cartairs Douglas）牧师来参与这项事工。是年4月14日下午，新街堂和竹树堂两堂外国牧师与会友122人聚集在新街堂，打马字主持，杜嘉德为主席，罗啻为推荐委员会委员，共同商议并差额选举了4位长老和4位执事（均为华人），并宣讲了教会管理方面的事宜。5月11日下午，教会在新街堂举行按立仪式，新任长老、长老正式走马上任。在厦门的宣教士的行为得到英国长老会的赞同，但却遭到了美国归正会总会的反对。因为他们觉得归正会与长老会是不同的宗派，难以很好共处。在厦门的罗啻、打马字等人立刻做出回应，他们认为美国归正会与英国长老会同属新教教会体系，并不存在巨大隔阂，相互同情，在教义上有共同的观点，在教会管理形式上也无分歧；而且中国人没有强烈的宗派、国籍的分辨。虽然他们的回应没有得到国内母会的认可，但他们仍然顶住压力，继续开展华人教会的自立运动。此后，厦门、漳州、泉州分设诸多堂会与支会，开枝散叶。
　　1862年4月2日，归正会和长老会正式成立了"厦门区会"。同年，在漳州白水营正式成立漳泉长老大会，又称"闽南长老会""漳泉大会""中国自治大会""中华基督教会"等。漳泉长老大会在1863年3月，按立罗嘉鱼和叶汉章为最早的华人牧师。1892年，漳属大会、泉属大会组成"漳泉长老总

会"。次年成立"闽南长老总会"。

英国伦敦会也在倡导华人教会自治，1872年，伦敦会的施敦力、马约翰、山雅各（James Sadler），与打马字、宣为霖（William Sutherland Swanson）、倪为霖（William Macgregor）、高休（Hugh Cowie）、叶汉章、蔡天乞等漳泉长老大会中外同工在泰山堂集会，一起按立黄承宜、林贞会为英国伦敦会在厦门的首任华人牧师。1873年2月22日，厦门伦敦会成立闽南联合大会，并进一步确定了教会管理原则，对信徒的文化素质、移风易俗等方面进行深入探讨，并分设厦门、漳泉两处和会。此次会议为日后闽南伦敦会的发展奠定了基础。1920年，在闽南的三公会同工在鼓浪屿举行会议，决议将闽南长老总会与伦敦会的和会联合起来建立闽南大会，共同管理闽南各地教务。其宗旨为联络闽南基督教会，合力进行，共图自养、自治、自传。参见：吴炳耀.百年来的闽南基督教会[M]//厦门文史资料(第13辑)，福建省厦门市文史资料委员会编印，1988；吴义雄.自立与本色化——19世纪末20世纪初基督教对华传教战略之转变 [J].中山大学学报(社会科学版)，2004(6)；吴保罗.闽南地区华人教会自立始末[N].福音时报，2018-04-01.——译者注

⑮ 萨米，塞缪尔的昵称。——译者注

⑯ 滚眼，又叫洗眼睛，剃头匠手艺之一。用左手拇指、食指撑开眼皮，将小银珠蘸了凉水，伸进眼中，在眼球及周边眼堂来回扒动。泪水微流却不痒不痛，只觉眼内轻松凉爽，十分自在。据说剃头匠中的高手可以滚眼治病。——译者注

⑰ 莫西，马西娅的昵称。——译者注

第四章　鼓浪屿散记

Chapter 4　Random Notes of Gulangyu

﹇Fun on Gulangyu﹈

We were taken almost daily for rambles on Kolongsu Island, or for a race on the hard sand of a strip of beach on the same side of the water that our house was facing. Our drawers were tucked up and we waded in the wavelets, or dug wells, just as children do today; only we did not don suits to go in the water much deeper than we did! That was unheard of in our day, for children or adults.

We owned a rowboat, and hired a Chinese boatman to care for it, and bring it to the wharf running along the side of our house, daily, or when desired. He did not pull the oars as we do in rowing, but stood up and pushed them, so he could face the bow; and it took a good deal of persuasion to get him to be willing to care for us and the boat, without eyes being painted on the

【乐在鼓浪屿】

我们几乎每天都被带去鼓浪屿上散步，或者在我家临海那一侧的一片硬沙滩上赛跑。我们挽起长裤裤脚，在微波细浪里蹚水，或者挖沙坑，就像今天的孩子们一样。只是我们没穿泳衣，不能到更深的水里去。泳衣在我们那个时代是闻所未闻的，无论是儿童还是成年人。

我们有一艘小船，雇了一名中国船夫来照看它，每天或有需要的时候，就把它拖到我们房子边的码头上。船夫不像我们划船时那样拉桨，而是站着摇橹，这样他就能面对船头了。苦口婆心劝了他半天，他才愿意照看我们和这条船。船的两侧没有按习俗画上眼睛，不像他们所有的舢板和小船那样。"没有眼睛，无法看路。"人们这样说。

我们几乎总是坐船去任何可能去的地方，一般去城外，但很少在城内逛街，因为那要面对极不卫生的环境，还有那么多举止粗鲁、行为丑陋的人盯着我们、骂我们。相反，也有许多人彬彬有礼，或者至少对我们很客气，不会对我们大喊大叫。

去沙滩玩耍的时候，母亲通常会坐在一块岩石上，照看着尚年幼的萨米或小马西娅，而父亲则和我们在岩石间嬉戏追逐，要么玩捉人游戏，要么捉迷藏。在一件令人震惊的事件发生在某些人身上后，我们变得非常害怕，不敢在岩石后面寻找父亲，直到他向我们保证没有危险，没有任何东西会伤害我们，才让我们安下心来。

孟加拉虎

一场大暴风雨过后，一艘船上的两名中国人看到有东西在游泳，他们以为是一条狗，就朝它划过去救它；但当它把爪子放在船沿儿，费劲爬进船舱时，他们看到的是一只孟加拉虎，长途跋涉从印度漂流到这里，已经筋疲力尽，因此暂时不会伤人。船夫尽快把船划到岸边，老虎急切地

bow, on either side, as is the custom with all their junks or boats. "No eyes; no see," they argued.

We almost always used the boat in going anywhere possible, out of the city, and rarely walked in the streets. There were so many unsanitary conditions to come up against, and rough, ugly-acting people who stared at us and called us names. There were, as well, reversely, many courteous ones, or at least quiet and civil to us.

Mother generally sat on a rock when at the beach, caring for Sammy or baby Marcia, in the younger days, while father romped with us, or played tag, or hide-and-seek, among the rocks. We grew quite frightened after a startling experience which came to some men, making us afraid to look behind rocks to find father, until he succeeded in assuring us there was no danger, and nothing would hurt us.

Bengal Tiger

After a heavy storm, two Chinamen in a boat saw what they thought was a dog swimming along and rowed toward it to save it aboard; but when it put claws on the edge and managed to scramble in, they saw it was a Bengal tiger, exhausted by its long drift from India, and so, harmless for the time. The men rowed to shore as soon as possible, but the tiger was as eager to escape to land, as they were to have it, and sprang to the shore and rushed to an old building not far in.

The men took courage, and had common sense enough to shut the door and brace it; then ran for help to a foreigner who had a gun. He climbed to the roof, and from there shot the animal, or there might have been terrible experiences, with a wild beast, famished and frightened, roaming loose in the thickly inhabited country about it!

Father's Company

There are numerous pictures in mind about rambles on Kolongsu Island, lying opposite the city on the mainland, about a mile's row across the water.

Father often ran with us, and frolicked in many ways. What a time Charley and I had learning the skip step, such as American children often took on the way to school, as we were told—and what they did, we wanted to do too, as an ideal always before us! We picked wild strawberries and raspberries that grew on hillsides, and other little fruits indigenous to the land, the taste and appearance of some of which is still clear.

想要逃到岸上，于是在他们即将到岸时，老虎一个弹跳落到岸上，接着冲进不远处一幢老房子里去了。

船夫鼓起勇气，依据常识判断，上前把门关上，并用棍子支住；然后跑去向一个有枪的外国人求助。他爬到屋顶上，从那里射杀了那只老虎；否则，一头饥饿受惊的野兽在这片人口稠密的土地上四处游荡，可能会成为人们可怕的梦魇。

父亲的陪伴

我的脑海里有很多关于在鼓浪屿上漫步的景象，小岛与大陆上的城市隔水相望，距离大约一英里。

父亲经常和我们一起跑步，做各种游戏。查理和我学会了跳步，是多么快乐啊！就像父亲跟我们说的，美国孩子在上学路上通常的样子——他们怎么做的，我们也想做，这是我们从未间断的理想！我们到山坡上采摘野草莓和树莓，还有一些土生土长的小果子，其中一些果子的味道和样子现在依然记得很清楚。

有一件让我胆战心惊却又必须要克服的事。在我们外出途经的小道上，经常拴着一头温顺的家养水牛。但对于我这个胆小的笨孩子来说，它那看上去凶神恶煞、盘旋张开的牛角实在让人怕得不得了。我总是请求不要带我从那里经过；每当途经此处，我走在父母中间时，恐惧得紧紧地抓住他们的手，不合时宜地尖叫。他们尝试各种方式让我克服恐惧：他们握紧我的手，安慰我，给我讲道理，甚至领着我，或者更有可能，是拖着我到水牛跟前，而养牛人家的孩子们则抚摸着它，和它玩耍，甚至被抱到牛背上去。通过说不清的综合因素，我终于开窍了，变得勇敢起来，能够在父母之间平静地走过水牛，不再发出叫喊声，而查理、萨米，以及后来的妹妹马西娅则毫无畏惧地在这只性情温和的水牛周围玩耍。

拜访领事

美国领事馆总办事处就在岛上，我们去拜访美国领事海雅先生，相谈甚欢，领事还向大人们介绍祖国的情况，但孩子们

I had to overcome one great terror. A gentle family buffalo was tethered near the path we often took to get beyond to other points, but those fierce looking spreading horns were too much for the foolishly timid child that I was. I begged always not to be taken past it, and clung with terror to both mother's and father's hands as I walked between them, screaming very unbecomingly! They tried every way they could to bring me out of my terror: by firmness and comforting and reasoning, and even leading, or probably, more likely dragging me near to the cow, while the Chinese children of the family who owned it, petted it, playing about it, and even were put on its back. My senses came to me at last through some combined influence and I grew brave enough to walk calmly between my parents, without an outcry, while Charley and Sam, and later Marcia frolicked around the gentle creature fearlessly!

Consuls Visited

We made calls on the American Consul, with Headquarters on the Island, Mr. Hyatt, with pleasant conversation and information about our Country's affairs among the grown-ups, which did not appeal to the children. We played with their son—an "American" boy about Charley's age—of whom we stood somewhat in awe, being of the order of our highest ideals; but if truth be told, should have been somewhat disillusioning, if we had not been so blind in our adoration of the species!

We also, on occasions, called on the Dutch Consul. I do not think there was the same cordiality between this Consulate, and the British and American ones, with father. Perhaps both remembered injustices perpetrated in the old Borneo days, which were embarrassments. However, once we had a wonderful time there, when the Consul ordered water and soap prepared for bubbles to be brought, and we were introduced to blowing bubbles "all colors of the rainbow'" while father and mother conversed in broken English with chatting and laughing, and then "tiffin" came in for all of us.

The British Consul had his headquarters on a high part of the city of Amoy, and calls there took us in another direction.

[Consul Doty]

Father acted as American Consul one year while Mr. Hyatt returned to his homeland

不感兴趣。我们和领事的儿子——一个和查理年龄相仿的"美国出生的"男孩一起玩，对他我们有些敬畏，因为他是我们最理想的典范。但是实话实说，如果我们对这种出身的人的崇拜不是那么盲目的话，他本应该让人有点美梦破灭的感觉。

有时，我们也去拜访荷兰领事。我认为荷兰领事不像英国和美国领事那样对父亲很热诚。也许两人都记得从前在婆罗洲时遭遇的不公正对待，有些尴尬。然而，有一次我们玩得很开心，领事叫人把吹泡泡用的水和肥皂准备好，然后教我们如何吹出五彩斑斓的彩虹泡泡；同时，他和父亲母亲用蹩脚的英语聊天，有说有笑，然后招待我们一顿简易午餐。

英国领事把他的总部设在厦门市区的高处，去拜访他们，我们要走另一个方向。

【罗啻领事】

有一年，父亲在海雅先生回国度假期间代理美国领事。我们房子上空飘扬着一面国旗，每天日出时升起，日落时降下。来自许多国家的生面孔来了又去，说了许多话，但我们那时太小，除了小有感触外，对那个时期的任何细节都不感兴趣，尽管在父亲的公文包里有许多他和其他人公务往来的信件。

一些英国朋友邀请我们去参加鼓浪屿上的一艘新船下水仪式，这可是一件相当了不起的事情。之后我们去了一个美丽的花园，花园里满是鲜花、蜿蜒的树篱和小径，看起来有点像古英格兰，都是这些英国人弄的。然后还要招待我们吃梅子蛋糕——毫无疑问，超级好吃，非常吸引孩子们，所以我们记住了！

船看起来又大又高，一路下滑，轰隆一声落水之后，在水中上下颠簸。船头、船尾和船舷上都挂满了旗帜。但我不记得是否有新船命名仪式。

【鼓浪屿传教士公墓 ①】

我们常常走去埋葬传教士的神圣之地。在墓地走路时，我们总是很轻柔、安

for a vacation. We had a flag flying over our house, to be raised at sunrise everyday, and hauled down at sunset. Strangers of many lands came and went, and there were many conversations; but we were too young to appreciate any details of that period, other than these little touches, though there are many copies of letters which passed between father and others on official business, among his folios.

Some English friends invited us to the launching of a boat from Kolongsu, which was quite an event, as afterwards we went into a lovely garden full of flowers and winding hedges and paths, made by these English people, to look like a bit of Old England. Then we were entertained with plum cake—plus—no doubt, but very appealing to the children and so remembered!

The boat looked large and high as it slid down the ways and bounced up and down in the water, after the first roar and splash—all bedecked with flags on bow and stern and from the sides! I do not recall a christening.

[Gulangyu Cemetery]

We often turned our steps toward the sacred Spot where the missionaries were buried. We always walked softly and quietly there, not jumping from one flat stone to another as we might on other occasions, while father and mother would linger by two little graves, and that of the mother, next to one of them; for all in this spot were dear ones, with a common bond of fellowship, who "held not their lives dear unto themselves."

"Man of War"

The officers of an American "Man of War", which was lying in the harbor, wanted a picnic on the other side of the Island near a Buddhist Temple. So mother and the other mission ladies and our Scotch and English friends joined in preparations. Boats from the Navy ships were used to row us over to the new spot, very picturesque, as I call it to mind, with garden and hills and rocks and dales and water.

Just the same preparations were made as always on other picnics we knew about, with a tablecloth spread on the grass, and good things to eat placed there in baskets and plates, and plenty of merry conversations and songs interspersed between informal offerings of food.

There were Navy officers with their brass buttons on caps and coats, and gold lace, and the rest of

静，不像在别的场合那样，从一块石板跳到另一块石板，而父亲和母亲会逗留在两个小坟墓旁，还有与其中之一毗连的其母亲的墓。因为长眠此处的皆是亲人，有着共同的志趣，他们"不把自己的生命据为己有"。

"勇士"号军舰来访

一艘美国军舰停靠在港口，"勇士"号上的军官想要在岛的另一边、离一座佛教寺庙不远的地方野餐。因此，母亲和其他传教女士们，还有我们的苏格兰和英格兰朋友都加入做饭工作中。海军军舰上放下来小船把我们送到野餐新营地，在我的记忆里，那里风景如画，有花园、小山、岩石、山谷和流水。

和我们所知道的其他野餐的准备工作一样，桌布铺在草地上，篮子和盘子里放着好吃的东西，人们开心地边吃边聊，又说又唱。

军官们戴着军帽，铜制纽扣熠熠闪亮，军大衣镶着金边，其余士兵戴着白色遮阳帽，穿着白色亚麻布套装；女士们穿着漂亮的平纹细布衣衫。我眼前依稀呈现出一幅画面：女士们戴着包头软帽，颏下系着带子，非常得体，就好像她们要去教堂一样正式，那时候的风俗是那样庄严肃穆。然而，我们不希望如此，我们还是希望微风吹过她们的头发，尽管头发会有点凌乱，但会让她们在热带的骄阳烈日下舒服许多。

【纽扣和寺庙】

参加聚会的一部分人去参观高处的寺庙，要爬很多台阶才能到达。我们这些孩子紧紧地拉着父母的手，对另一种信仰的神职人员感到一丝恐惧，面对着我们的是一尊面容凶恶的神像。我们进了寺庙，这时有一个和尚拦住我们，说要给神灵献祭才行。有人捐了钱，但他说这还不够，他们的神灵想要一些军装上亮闪闪的纽扣。军官们不同意，和他争执起来，也许是他们相当傲慢，始终不肯退让。他们试图从和尚身边绕过去，但被和尚执拗地挡住。

the men in pith helmets and white linen suits, and the ladies in pretty muslins. A dim picture comes before me, that the ladies wore bonnets tied down under their chins as properly as if they were going to church, so dignified were the customs of those days. However, let us hope not, but rather, that the breeze blew through their hair, disheveling it somewhat and making them far more comfortable under the tropical skies!

[Buttons & the Temple]

Some of the party visited the Temple on a high prominence, with many steps to climb to reach it. We children held father's and mother's hands tightly, a little fearsome of priests of another faith, and a big idol with fierce countenance which faced us. We entered the Temple, when a priest stopped us, saying an offering to their god was expected. Money was offered, but he said that would not suffice; their god wanted some of those bright buttons! The officers demurred and argued, and probably were rather arrogant and insistent in refusing. They started to walk past the priest, but were as insistently held back for the buttons. Finally, not very graciously I guess, one of the officers whipped out his knife and cut off one or two and handed them to the company of priests who had gathered by this time. They blandly and suavely received them and allowed us to pass.

Probably I never would have entered a Buddist Temple but for this episode. I do not seem to remember any impression of the interior, or what occurred there, other than to look upon the great idol, with forbidding face.

Chinese Interiors

There is another episode of my life in Amoy connected with Chinese interiors, which I am glad I had, though at the cost of being a naughty child!

We were always forbidden to go out on the street alone. Once or twice a little Chinese girl who lived on the opposite side of the street from us, called to me to come over and play with her. I remember her face was all covered with white spots—small pox—and in their unsanitary life, no care was ever taken to protect anyone from it!

I had wandered into the nurses' quarters, and was very positively prevented from going over, at this time by old Boa. But again I was coaxed from across the street, and no one saw me as, alas!

最后，一个军官并不优雅地抽出他的刀，割下一个或两个纽扣，交给此时聚拢来的和尚们。和尚们和蔼而又温文尔雅地接过去，并给我们放行。

要不是这一插曲，我可能永远也不会进佛教寺庙。我对寺庙内部的印象或里面发生了什么事似乎记不起了，只记得仰头望着那尊巨大的神像，面容狰狞，令人生畏。

中国人家内部

我在厦门的生活中还有一段与中国人家有关的经历，尽管代价是当了一回淘气包，但我还是很高兴我有这番经历。

我们外国孩子总是被禁止单独上街。有一两回，住在街对面的一个中国小女孩叫我过去和她一起玩。我记得她脸上满是白色斑点——天花，她们生活环境不卫生，从来没有采取措施保护别人免受传染。

我一度溜达进保姆们的住处，这时老保姆态度明确，不让我过去。但我又一次禁不住穿过马路的诱惑，而且当我溜下楼梯时，啊！竟然没人看见我！我溜出去到街上，然后穿过马路。之后我被带到楼上，房间里又黑又臭，烟雾弥漫，屋里全是人，男男女女的，好奇地打量我的穿着，上上下下看个遍。这里也有一尊面目凶恶的神像在看着我，我开始害怕了，这时有人来找我——我想是那个保姆，她已经有一会儿没看见我了。我回想起家里人似乎满怀恐惧，因为我曾暴露在传染病区；人们听说绑架时有发生，我有可能会孤零零地被关在地窖子里，而且没人知道我还会遇到什么别的事情。

我被带回家了，不过这些中国人对于我被带走，除了愤怒的嚷嚷之外，我不记得他们还有什么抗议举动。守护天使一直照看着我，没有让我受到伤害。我父母训斥我的方式一定是想让我牢记，我做了一件多么可怕的事情，但奇怪的是我脑子里除了一种敬畏感之外，什么概念也没有，而且再也没有朝街对面那个小女孩看一眼。对我来说，由于事件的结局很幸运，也没发生什么意外，所以我敢于回首往事，看到一幅普通苦力家庭阴郁凄凉的景象，它

I slipped down stairs and out on the street and across. I was taken upstairs, where the room was dark and smoky and smelly, and full of men and women who were curious to examine my clothes and everything about me. There was a fierce idol, too, looking at me, and I was beginning to be afraid, when someone came for me—I think the nurse, who had missed me for a few moments. I recall the terror everyone seemed to feel, that I had been so exposed to contagion; and there were known to be kidnappings, sometimes, when I might have been switched off to some underground place, and no one knows what else might have come to me.

But I was brought home with no consciousness of any further protest from the Chinese people than angry words that I had been taken away from them. I had been watched over by guardian angels, and no harm had come to me. My parents must have dealt with me in a way that impressed it upon me what a dreadful thing I had done, but, strangely, I have nothing defined in mind but a sense of awesomeness over me, and never again even looked across the way to the little girl. So, since it ended mercifully for me, and all was well, I can look back to a vision of gloom and forlornness as the ordinary home of coolie people, which should stir a heart of pity for the wretchedness of many lives in that land, for whose uplift and release from evil conditions, father and mother had devoted their lives, in His Name.

[Sampans in the Rain]

The numberless rowboats which we saw from our windows were, many of them, homes of coolie families,—living in one end, having a low bamboo cabin or tent over it, which sheltered it from sun and beating rain; while, on a little brazier in the open front, their rice was cooked—their only food, and not much of it either.

We could see this housekeeping going on from our upstairs windows, and 0! It did look so good. I just longed to get under that bamboo covering and have rain patter down all about me, while I sat, dry, within, and watched it! This was a recurring longing; and even to this day I find myself recalling the little bamboo protection from rain, and thrilling as I sit under shelter and watch it patter or downpour about me.

The typhoons, which came in season, were very disastrous to those poor little boats, with their teeming families cooped up in them.

会激起一颗怜悯之心，同情这片土地上人们的不幸，而父母以上帝的名义，献出了自己的生命，为的是使他们得到升华，把他们从悲惨境地中拯救出来。

【雨中的舢板】

我们窗口外可以看见无数桨划的小船，其中许多船就是苦力的家，船的一头住人，上面罩着低矮的竹篷或棚屋，可以遮阳避雨；而在船头露天的小火炉上，是他们做的米饭——他们唯一的食物，量也不多。

我们从楼上窗户可以看到船家忙着打理家务，哦，看起来确实很不错。我真想钻到竹篷下面，让雨水在我周围拍打，而我却干干爽爽地坐在里面，看着雨落！这种渴望萦绕不去，甚至直到今天，我还会想起那遮雨的小竹篷，激动地坐在雨篷下，看着雨滴淅淅沥沥或哗哗啦啦地从四面八方落下来。

季节性的台风对那些可怜的小船来说可是灾难，鸽笼般的船上挤了全家人。海滩上散落着失事船只的残骸和失去的生命。这些台风带给我们仅有的几天寒冷的日子，只是偶尔而已。于是，寒冷的日子烤一场炉火让我们很激动，尽情绕着敞开炉栅的煤火跳来跳去，看着蓝色和金色的火苗噼噼啪啪地燃烧——这对父母来说，也有种"昔日重来"的感觉。

【许多国家的船只】

　　偶尔，我和查理陪着父母去拜访英国和美国船的舰长，以及他们时而随行的妻子，还有其他国家的舰长。我们被邀请到他们的舰长室——根据舰船的级别或他们所属的国家，有的宽敞、漂亮，有的窄小、肮脏。即使在那个时候也是"不列颠称霸海上"，英国船上一切都井井有条，尽管与英国舰船相比，我们的数量少得可怜，但我们的船上一切也有条不紊。东印度人、荷兰人、暹罗人或波斯人的船都凌乱不堪。

　　他们总是拿葡萄酒和梅子蛋糕招待我们。有一次，我记得是一艘法国船，给了我们一个装饰得很精致，让孩子眼馋不已

The beaches were then strewn with wrecks and lives lost. These typhoons brought our only cold days, and occasionally. Then the event of having an open fire caused excitement among us, and we all made the most of hovering over the coals in the open grate, watching the blue and gold flames as they crackled—a bit of "auld lang syne" to father and mother this was, too.

[Ships of Many Nations]

Occasionally, Charley and I accompanied our parents when they were calling on the Captains of British and American ships, and on their wives, who sometimes came with them, or on those of other nationalities; and were invited down into their staterooms—large and handsome, or small and grimy, according to the class of vessel, or the nation they belonged to. "Britannia ruled the waves" even then too, and everything on their ships was in fine order, and on ours too, though they were few and far between compared to the British ones. An East Indiaman, or Dutch or Siamese or Persian craft would be unkempt.

We were always offered wine and plum cake. One time a French vessel, I think, offered us a much decorated cake which took a child's eye—little figures of people and animals, gaily colored, covered the top. We could not understand their language, nor they ours, and we had a funny time. The British "Men of War" came oftenest to our harbor, and sometimes returned after various trips up and down the coast, so our parents grew to know their commanders. There were warm and cordial greetings and social times among them, also with our own men, oftener than among other nationalities.

Among souvenirs which mother evidently enjoyed keeping, is a package of calling cards from Captains or officers with titles, and "H.M.S." or "U.S.A," in the corners; and cards from consuls of different nations, and other dignitaries also, interesting to look over, after all these years.

One occasion or two stand out in my memory. The officers took pleasure in entertaining us children, and showed us over parts of the ship and brought out monkeys and parrots and other treasures. They asked if we would like to fish down the hold with hook and line, and said we would surely catch something, which filled us with great excitement. We were told to toll out the line given us as far down as we could, and if we felt a bite, pull up quickly; and sure enough,

的蛋糕——蛋糕上面绘着色彩鲜艳的人物和动物图案。我们听不懂法语，他们也听不懂英语，但我们都很开心。英国的"勇士"号最经常来访厦门港，有时在沿海走南闯北的航行后泊靠厦门，所以父亲母亲和他们的指挥官逐渐熟悉了。比起其他国家的船员，英国人和美国人更经常地给我们热烈而又亲切的问候，并举行社交活动。

母亲喜欢保留的纪念品中，有一盒子名片，这些年来，她总是饶有兴趣地翻看。名片上面写着舰长或军官的头衔，名片一角印着英国皇家海军舰艇的首字母缩写"HMS"或美国缩写"USA"等字样；还有来自不同国家领事和其他达官显贵的名片。

在我的记忆中，有一两件事印象突出。军官们以款待我们这些孩子为乐，带我们参观军舰的各个舱室，还拿出猴子、鹦鹉和其他宝贝。他们问我们是否愿意到下舱去用鱼钩和鱼线钓鱼，并信誓旦旦地保证我们肯定能钓到什么，这使我们极其兴奋。他们告诉我们要尽可能地把线往下甩出，

中国故事
——罗嘉女儿回忆厦门生活（1851—1859）

The China Story
—Recollections of a Little Girl's Life in Amoy.
China (1851—1859)

如果感到咬钩了，就迅速拉上来；果然，我们钓到东西了——但不是一条鱼，而是一袋方糖、一些坚果或饼干！这一切对我们来说都是非常愉快和神秘的，我们一直玩到不得不被人叫走才离开军舰。

还有一次，舰长叫炮手们给一门重炮装上炮弹，要鸣炮欢迎我们。用推弹杆前装弹式的大炮属于过去那个时代，巨大的炮弹就在我们眼前，金字塔般堆在甲板上，这时我受到惊吓，只会可怜兮兮地呜咽哭泣，恳求舰长不要开炮。他和颜悦色地笑了笑，迁就我，叫他的士兵退下。从对我的关心来看，我一定是一个被宠坏了的孩子，也是我的"绅士朋友们"娇惯的人。

有一天，查理和我受邀上船吃午饭。至于是谁邀请，为什么邀请，是单独邀请我们还是与父母一起受邀等细节，我不记得了，但一件小事这些年来一直没忘。比我大两岁的查理因餐桌上没有餐前祷告很是震惊，并说了出来，问为什么不祷告，这让舰长很尴尬，舰长支支吾吾地问查理是否会做祷告，然后查理就背诵了一遍《主祷文》。

我想起了一幅母亲梳妆打扮准备赴

we caught something—not a fish, though, but a bag of lump sugar or some nuts or cookies! It was all very delightful and mysterious to us, and lasted until we had to be called off to leave the ship.

Another time, the Captain called on the gunners to load up one of their heavy cannon, and give us a salute. Great cannon balls were in our sight, piled up in pyramids on the deck, and ramrods were used—all belonging to a past age, in this form—when what did poor little terrified "Pussie" do, but sob and cry, and plead with the Captain not to fire. He humored me with a good natured laugh, and called off his men! I must have been quite a spoiled child, as well as a pet, with my "gentlemen friends", from the attentions shown to me.

One day Charley and I were invited to lunch on a vessel. I do not remember any detail as to who asked us, or why, or if alone or with our parents, but an instance has persisted all these years. Charley—two years older than I—was quite shocked because no "blessing" was asked at the table, and expressed it, asking why not, to the embarrassment of the Captain, who parried by asking if he could say it and he repeated the "Lord's Prayer"!

A picture of mother preparing to go out on these calls, or other occasions, comes to mind, I, standing by the side of her bureau and looking up at her "tying her bonnet under her chin"—a white one sent in one of the boxes from home, indistinctly, I can see, decorated with pink ribbons, or it may have been flowers; O! So pretty, I thought— and then throwing a Cashmere shawl over her shoulders, laying the folds "just so" over a black satin dress; then kissing me goodbye, the times I did not go too. Sometimes she wore a grey silk, or a grey striped gown, which did not appeal to a five or six years old child, who only had eyes for something gay like the shawl or hat!

[Parsees]

Parsees from way off India way, came occasionally to call, while on their commercial trips to China and Amoy, and once, one brought mother a beautiful silver and blue satin dress material; and again a gauze one, wide striped, of gold and blue colors, which looked as if it might grace a Hindoo lady of high degree, if in its native setting.

I received, also, a large sample book of India prints of different colors on the well-known red background, each sample about one quarter yard square, which were

约，还是什么别的场合的情景。我站在她衣橱旁，抬头看着她把包头软帽系在下巴底下——帽子是白色的，用箱子从美国寄来的，我依稀看见它装饰着粉红色丝带或者是花朵。哦，我觉得太漂亮了——然后，母亲在肩上披上一条开司米披肩，胸前打褶，恰到好处地盖在一件黑缎连衣裙上。我不跟母亲同去的时候，母亲会吻我告别。有时她穿一件灰色的丝质长裙或灰色的条纹长裙，这对一个五六岁的孩子来说没什么吸引力，他们只对鲜艳的披肩或帽子感兴趣。

【帕西人】

来自遥远印度的帕西人，借助来厦门商业旅行的时机，偶尔来拜访我们。有一次，有人给母亲带来了一件漂亮的银色和蓝色缎子衣服布料。又有一件纱罗，带着金黄色和蓝色的宽条条纹，如果是在它的故乡印度，似乎可以使一个印度贵妇更加优雅。

我也得到了一大本印度印花棉布样品册，彩色的棉布印在著名的红色背景上，每个布片大约四分之一码见方，都是我随时从剪刀下，母亲在世时的针线活，还有到了美国后，从外祖母和玛丽阿姨手中积攒下来的，尽管当时没有充分体恤到恩情，现在回想起来却是不胜感激。因此，我现在就有一床华丽的被子，上面印着永不褪色的印度红白印花，作为那个时刻的永恒纪念。

【中国访客】

父母接待了许多中国男人，也亲自接待中国妇女来访。上至戴着孔雀翎官帽、穿着刺绣的真丝锦缎袍、地位高贵的官员，中有士绅，下至卑微的农夫，来访者分别按照自己的身份行礼问候。他们对我们奇异的风俗、外貌和陈设都满怀兴趣和好奇心，对钢琴惊叹不已，弹琴唱歌，品尝我们用于招待的美式蛋糕，还有用中国陶瓷杯子盛的茶。

父亲喜欢搞恶作剧。他以前遇到的一些人有一次来拜访他，他准备了一碗水，放进去电线，碗底放了一块银圆。他说谁能把银圆捡起来，就归谁。但是，啊！结

rescued from my ever-ready scissors and needle by mother, in her day, and by my grandmother and aunt Mary, after the sample book had found its way to America—many thanks in retrospect—though not so graciously considered at the time! And in consequence, I have a gorgeous quilt of never fading Indian red prints combined with white, as a lasting memento of that occasion.

[Chinese Visitors]

Father and mother received many calls from Chinese men, and also, by themselves, from the women. Gentlemen of rank, with their peacock feather in hat and embroidered gowns of silk and satin, down through the lower ranks to the humble peasant, came with courtesies, according to their positions. They were all filled with interest and curiosity over our strange customs and appearance and furnishings, and marveled at the piano, and playing on it and singing, and were served with American cakes and tea from their own kind of porcelain cups.

Father enjoyed a practical joke, and during one of these calls from people he had met before, he prepared some electrical wiring in a bowl of water with a piece of silver coin in the bottom. He offered to give the coin to anyone who could pick it out, but lo! The electric shock caught him. Then he wanted one of his friends to catch it, with the same result, of course. They all wished to try for it, however, and it caused astonishment among them. Then and there father gave them the first elemental lesson on the existence, use and power of electricity, very simply known about and used, at best, in that early day!

A missionary has to be a "Jack of all trades", and father took with him a set of dentistry instruments, and used to give help and relief as best he could to many of the foreigners, who considered it "better than nothing", anyway! These instruments were a source of great interest to skilled Chinamen, of whom of course, we know there were many, as they handled them carefully. His chest of fine tools also, they admired and praised.

The women never accompanied the men, but were as eager to visit mother. Some were acquaintances, and even friends; others, entire strangers, as it was with the men. Their curiosity took more feminine forms, and more equal to their supposed capacity of minds. Mother played and sang for them; that was always asked for, by those who knew about it, and they appreciated this, anyway.

果触电了！于是，他让他的一个朋友伸手取银圆，结果当然是同样的下场。然而，朋友们都想试一试，只落得惊讶不已。就在此时此地，父亲给大家上了第一堂关于电的存在、使用和电能的基础课，那个时候，人们对电的认识和使用充其量也是非常简单不过。

一个传教士必须是一个多面手。父亲带了一套牙科器械，常常尽其所能地帮助外国人减轻病痛，他们认为这不管怎样都"聊胜于无"。这些器械对中国工匠来说吸引力无边，当然，我们知道中国工匠人数众多，他们操作时小心翼翼。父亲那装着精细工具的箱子也受到他们的钦羡与赞赏。

中国女人从不陪同她们男人来访，但她们也同样渴望去拜访母亲。有些是相识的人，甚至是朋友；其他人则完全是陌生人，就像男人们一样。女人们的好奇心以更女性化的形式出现，也与她们该有的智力更为匹配。那些知道母亲善于唱歌的人，总是请求母亲为她们弹琴和唱歌，不管怎样，她们还是很感激的。

母亲把衣服拿给她们看，衣服缝纫法和她们的很不一样。有一次，一个女人问母亲能否把手给她看一下，并抓起母亲的左手食指，看看上面是否有针眼。她很高兴地发现母亲有，因为有共同的优越的文化和她们编织的精美刺绣，手上的针眼就成了中国女人之间的纽带，也成了她们与我母亲之间的纽带。母亲是她们相当喜欢的外国女人。但是，母亲的天足很难让人接受：她的脚那么大，没裹足——就像苦力的脚，或者像道德败坏的女人的脚！没有哪个淑女会留这样的脚，她们的裹脚小巧玲珑，穿着色彩鲜艳的丝绸或天鹅绒质地的刺绣精美的鞋子，而母亲穿的是黑色皮鞋。不过，还是个性赢得了胜利，母亲被视为可以来往的同伴；否则，如果这位中国女士没有认同感，她就不会来看母亲。女人们一起喝茶，所用的茶杯如此精致，连法国瓷器厂也无可精进！吃着美国蛋糕、水果，或磅蛋糕，或简单的拼盘，她们愉快地聊天。一般来说，我们这些孩子不会坐很长时间，没法儿弄懂她们说什么，所以对她们的谈话内容没有留下任何印象。

She showed them her dresses, made so differently from theirs, however! Once, a woman asked if she could see, and took up her left forefinger to see if there were needle pricks over it. She was quite delighted to find them—a bond between themselves, with their superior culture, and the wonderful embroidery which they could do—a bond with this foreign woman, whom they rather liked. But the feet were hardly to be accepted. Hers were so big, and unbound—just like coolie feet, or those of the immoral woman! No lady would ever wear such, and theirs were tiny and bound, with shoes exquisitely embroidered in beautiful colors on silk or velvet, while hers were just made of black leather. Still, personality won, and she was received as one to be associated with as an equal; or, if the Chinese lady felt otherwise, she stayed away from visiting her. They had their cup of tea also, in the dainty cups of their own kind, which could not be improved upon from factories in France! American cake, fruit or pound cake, or simple jumbles were offered and they chatted away for some time with pleasure. Generally we children could not sit still long enough to absorb ideas of what was said, so nothing is retained of their conversation.

[Writing Letters Home]

About once a month, father would bring home from his morning's work, to mother, word that a ship carrying American mail would sail in a few days, or even less. Then intensive writing was the main occupation of both of them, to gather together what had been written through the month, with present additions; letters "home" always, and to many friends and relatives, or official reports to the "Board of Foreign Missions", or other public matters. Then we children were quite neglected, and banished to the care of the two nurses. If we ventured to steal into the room where mother sat at her Chinese lacquered desk, with pen rapidly scratching up and down, as we thought, and ventured to ask a question, her hand would go out, and her voice said, "No, children, you must not disturb me. Mother will answer after the mail leaves."

We knew it was final and crept away, longing for letter time to stop and we could be with her again. We never ventured into father's study, I guess. This was a frequent memory, as letters were faithfully and lov-

【写家书】

大约一个月一次，父亲会从早上工作中带话儿回家，告诉母亲，一艘发往美国的邮船将在几天内甚至更短的时间内起航。于是，他们两个人的主要工作就是密集写信，把这一个月里写的东西收到一起，再添加上一些新的内容。给家人的信是必备的，还有给众多亲朋好友的信，或给海外差传理事会的正式报告，或其他有关公共事务的信件。既然是这样，我们这些孩子就被完全忽视了，被放逐到两个保姆那里去照顾。如果我们冒险溜进母亲的房间，就像我们想的那样，她坐在她那张中国漆制书桌前，奋笔疾书，如果我们大着胆子问个问题，她会伸手阻止说："不，孩子们，你们不要来打扰我。信寄出后，妈妈会回答你们的问题。"

我们知道这是不可更改的，便蹑手蹑脚地走了，渴望着写信时间早点结束，我们就可以再和母亲在一起了。我想我们从来没敢进父亲的书房。记忆中，这样的事屡屡出现，因为在这十一年里，父亲和母亲都准时准点地写信，满怀慈爱，后来母亲去世后，就剩下父亲一个人按时给外祖母写信，正如外祖母忠实而深情地回信一样。

母亲的挚友

两位陪丈夫来回奔波做茶业生意的女士，与父母结下了深厚的友谊。她们是英格兰的包义德太太和苏格兰的赛姆太太，她俩分别来自伦敦与爱丁堡。与包义德太太的关系也许更亲近些，只要母亲需要朋友时，比如生孩子的时候，她就会来帮母亲；反过来，在包义德太太的孩子相继夭折时，母亲也会去安慰和帮助她。

在一次远离厦门的旅行中，赛姆先生和太太去美国访问，并到外祖父母家里看望，给他们带去了很多欢乐，讲述了许多关于母亲和孩子们厦门生活的细节。当他们再次返回厦门的时候，带回最新消息给我们，有关许多朋友的现状，有什么事情发生，有些什么变化，这些都被外祖父母指出一定"要告诉埃莉诺相关的一切"。

ingly written through those eleven years by both father and mother, and after that, as faithfully sent by the one left, to the mother, and as loyally and affectionately replied to by grandmother.

Mrs. Boyd & Mrs. Syme

Two ladies who accompanied their husbands in their trips back and forth in the tea trade, formed warm friendships with both of our parents. They were Mrs. Boyd of England, and Mrs. Syme of Scotland, London and Edinburgh. Mrs. Boyd was perhaps the more intimate, and came to mother, and she to her, whenever a friend was needed, as in birth of babies, and in Mrs. Boyd's case, in the death of hers—none ever living—and mother would go to her to give comfort and assistance.

In one of the trips away from Amoy, Mr. and Mrs. Syme visited America, and came to our grandparents' home, bringing much joy in being able to tell many details of mother's life and of her children; and when they returned again to Amoy, brought latest words of many friends, and things and changes, which had been pointed out to them "to tell Eleanor about".

When I was between five and

64

six years old, Mrs. Boyd invited me to spend every Friday with her, she sending her beautiful boat, much like a gondola, for me and returning me home again. I had lovely visits with her, and she did things to interest and entertain a little child, evidently giving up her time to me when there.

There were three English missionaries and their families in our midst. I wish I understood what their work was as related to father and other Americans. Evidently they worked in a friendly way, and were warm friends as it seemed to a little child. They were under an English mission and direction, and had other work, though I remember their men and father often in earnest conversation together, in one home or the other.

We children more often went to the home of father's associates where there were children—to Mr. Talmage's, who went out for the first time on the same ship with them. I remember there were happy times among us as we spent "days" together, going home late afternoons. We went to Kolongsu together or to the beach and romped, while the parents visited more quietly, though, Mr. Talmage and father both had a love of fun, and humor, and all had cheery conversation.

在我五六岁的时候，每个星期五，包义德太太都邀请我和她一起过，她派她那艘漂亮的小船来接我，很像平底的贡多拉船，然后再送我回家。我去她那里愉快地做客，她和我做一些有趣的游戏，哄我开心；很显然，我每次到她那里玩，她都用全部时间陪伴我。

我们中间有三个英国传教士和他们的家人。他们的工作与父亲和其他美国人的工作如何相关，我希望我能理解。显然，他们很友好地合作，在我这个小孩子看来，是热情的朋友。他们受某个英国差会的派遣和指导，而且还有别的工作，我记得他们和父亲经常你来我往，真诚地交谈。

我们这些孩子更经常去父亲的同事打马字先生的家，他家也有孩子。打马字先生第一次离家来华时与父母乘坐同一条船。我记得我们在一起的日子，总是傍晚才回家，度过了快乐的时光。我们一起去鼓浪屿或海滩嬉戏玩耍。尽管双方父母的拜访更为安静，不过打马字先生和父亲都风趣幽默，总是相谈甚欢。

【第一次厦门国际基督教团契 ②】

有一间外国教堂，或者说是一个房间，专门用来举行礼拜仪式，所有牧师轮流来主持讲坛。除了要为中国人举行礼拜活动之外，我们定期参加团契。年轻的茶商也常去，我有一张画像，是他们中间一个人画我团契时睡着的情景并送给了我，这让我极度尴尬。事后不久，当他来访的时候，我试图躲着他，仍然觉得自己做了一件多么可怕的事，而母亲脸上的微笑，加上他的话，仍然留在我的记忆里。

有一年，我陪父亲走在城里的大街上，去给熟识的华人拜年，这是他们的阴历新年，不是我们的新年。我们走进一位先生的房子，里面有雕刻精美的凳子、椅子和木制隔板，镶板上还有非常精美的图画。我们受到极热烈的欢迎。最引我注目的是他们拱起双手作揖的方式。当然，关于谈话的主旨，我也不懂，只是忙着看雕刻品、镶板和绘有图案的白色席子。但当精致的

[The First XICF—Xiamen International Christian Fellowship]

There was a foreign church, or room, fitted out for services, and all ministers took turns in filling the pulpit. We regularly attended there, except those otherwise engaged in services with the Chinese. Our young tea merchants were often there, and I have a picture one of them drew of me asleep, and sent to me, which caused deep mortification. I tried to hide from him, when he called shortly after, and proceeded to make me feel what a dreadful thing I had done, while the smile on mother's face, in conjunction with his words, stays in my memory yet!

One year I accompanied father through the streets of the city, as he made New Year's calls on acquaintances among the Chinese—on their Day, not ours. We went into one gentleman's house in which were beautiful carved stools and chairs and woodwork in partitions, and very delicate painting in panels. We were most cordially received. The manner of shaking one's own hands stands out before me. Of the purport of conversation, of course, I know nothing, but was busy looking at the carvings and panels and figured white mattings; but when dainty plates of candles and cakes were passed, I had eyes for them! We went to a store, where were piles of beautiful, colored silks and embroideries, and father and the merchants chatted together with laughter at times, then passing of more cakes and candies.

In going in the streets, we came to a long flight of stone steps—a part of the street, though not leading up to a temple as we often see in pictures of Oriental countries. We trudged up these to the British Consulate. Interesting conversation passed between the Consul and father, but I did not receive any attention here, I remember; and that has always stayed with me!

The Sedan was the only mode of ordinary travel at that early day, other than walking, in the parts that I knew anything about—pictures of other portions of the Empire showed other modes, I know.

Father took me in one to the Chinese church—my only trip ever taken in a sedan, as also my only time in a native Christian church, and with father as the preacher.

The men sat on one side and women on the other; and they sang some of our familiar hymns, to words in their own tongue. It did not seem pleasant, to the child who was used to sweet tones, but,

蜡烛和糕饼端上来时，我的眼睛就盯着不放了。我们去了一家商店，里面有一摞摞漂亮的鲜艳丝绸和刺绣品，父亲和店主们聊着天，不时地大笑，然后他们又递给我们更多的糕饼和糖果。

走在街上，我们来到了一长段石头台阶，这是街道的一部分，但没有通向寺庙，不像我们在东方国家的照片中经常看到的那样。我们费力地爬上台阶，到了英国领事馆。领事和父亲聊天，兴致很浓，但我记得在这里没人管我，让我耿耿于怀。

在以前那个时代，就我所知的厦门一带，除了步行，轿子是唯一的寻常旅行方式——我知道，有照片显示清帝国其他地区还有其他的方式。

父亲曾带我坐轿子去中国教堂，而这是我唯一一次坐轿子，也是我唯一一次上当地的基督教堂，父亲在那里当牧师。

男女分坐两边，他们用自己的语言唱着我们熟悉的赞美诗。对于我这样一个习惯了英语甜美音调的孩子来说，他们的唱诗似乎并不太好听，但毫无疑问，颂赞的目的已经达到。教堂又黑又暗又臭！但是，即使在那时，建造一所舒适教堂的计划已经启动了，作为敬拜上帝的殿堂。我们参加了教堂的奉献仪式。

随着年龄的增长，查理和我开始明白为什么我们的父母会在这片土地上，以及他们总是在忙些什么，这与我们小时候的理解不同。

without doubt filled its purpose. The church was dark and dingy and smelly! But plans for a pleasant house were under way, even then, and we attended the dedication of it, as a house of God and Worship.

As we grew older, Charley and I began to understand why our parents were in this land and what they were constantly busy about, differently from the comprehension of our younger days.

【注释】

① 鼓浪屿传教士公墓：鼓浪屿内厝澳崎仔尾，俗称内厝澳"十八脚桶"排屋的西面，隔着马路围有一片墓园，这片墓园不同于鼓浪屿龙头俗称"番仔墓"的洋人墓园。番仔墓是一处供来厦外国人共用的墓地，而传教士公墓纯属在厦门传教的英美基督教3个差会专有的。这里排列着60个墓位，这一片墓园处于现编为内厝澳路217号的地块中，原有的地块面积2237平方米，纵横约47米，如今却仅剩下守墓人小屋的一隅。故事讲到此时此刻，此地埋葬着罗啻的3个亲人：长子费里斯（1844年7月19日在厦门去世）、首任妻子克拉丽莎（1845年10月5日病逝）、第二任妻子所生7个月大的男婴爱德华（Edward Smith Doty，1848年7月14日去世）。作者和父母亲就是来探看这三人。后来作者的母亲、罗啻牧师第二任妻子于1858年2月28日去世，享年34岁。再后来还有罗啻牧师4个月大的女儿埃尔迈拉（Elmira Louisa Doty）葬于此处。（叶克豪：《鼓浪屿内厝澳崎仔尾传教士公墓文献考证》，《鼓浪屿研究（第八辑）》，北京：社会科学文献出版社，2018年，第162页）——译者注

② 团契，即伙伴关系，源自《圣经》中的"相交"一词，意思为相互交往

和建立关系，是指上帝与人之间的相交以及基督徒之间相交的亲密关系。团契现在常用作基督教（新教）特定聚会的名称，其旨在增进基督徒和慕道友共同追求信仰的信心和相互分享、帮助的集体情谊。因而广义的团契也可指教会和其他形式的基督徒聚会。团契生活是基督徒最基本的和非常重要的教会生活，所以团契也被称为基督徒团契。——译者注

第五章 父母的成就、孩子的成长和当地的习俗

Chapter 5 Accomplishments of Parents, Growth of Kids, and Local Customs

【《翻译英华厦腔语汇》】

传教士们迫切地想把《圣经》的部分章节和做礼拜用的赞美诗翻译成当地的语言，也想编纂一本自己的厦门方言字典。整个中国有许多方言，在帝国内方言互不相通。随着时间推移，这些传教士也渴望给自己的新教堂留下一些文献。我们收集的父亲的译作中，有一本《翻译英华厦腔语汇》，编纂者赫然写着父亲的名字。我们手中的字典中某些部分是母亲的手迹。

一个又一个传教士，包括英国传教士，不停地在印刷室忙着，要么翻译，要么编纂书籍，再交给装订工。我想这些中国人的印刷手艺一定很高超，因为所有的书籍和小册子都符合制作工艺。当然，书籍是

[Amoy Dictionary]

The missionaries were eager to translate parts of the Bible into their own language, and hymns for their services, and also to complete a dictionary of their own dialect used in Amoy. There are many dialects in the whole of China, no one of which is understood by the rest of the people of the Empire. These workers also desired to give their new church some literature too, as time went on. One Manual of their dialect—bearing father's name as compiler—is in our collection of his Translations. There is also some work in this line in mother's handwriting, which we have.

One or another of the missionaries, including the British ones, were busy in the printing press room continually, in traslating or compiling books for the bookbinders; who I think must have been Chinese men of skill in that line, as all the books and pamphlets are according to their workmanship, and, of course, being for their use, begin at what we would call at the end of the works!

I recall the pleasure, one time expressed, when someone brought a new book in to show us all—finished at last, and so well and artistically done—and the relief and joy over its accomplishment. The press room was not at our home. Father's life was a busy one. He was a very methodical man, and regularly went out after breakfast—dressed, generally, in white linen clothes and pith helmet—so often used in the Tropics—into Chinese homes, or for printing work, or in preaching or teaching, or to meet with others in this work in earnest conversation and planning.

There were times when father and the others went on journeys into the interior, and were away for several days. Two generally made the tours together, and after the work was established, native elders accompanied them. Travel by water was more desirable whenever possible, and the Mission owned a sailboat and oars combined, which was used on these trips. Itineraries required provisioning with bedding and food and medicine, as well as boxes of books and leaflets to be distributed to members in established centers, or to new ones who showed an interest in having them.

All our family were very glad when father returned; and there was much eager and earnest conversation, which we children were

印给他们用，所以从一开始就达到我们所说的做到了极致。

当有人拿进来一本最终完成、制作精美、很有艺术感的新书给大家看时，我回想起人们一度表现出的那种快乐，如释重负的成就感与兴奋。印刷室不在我们家里。父亲的生活很忙碌，他也是一个很有条理的人，照常在早饭后外出。一般是穿着热带地区常用的白色的亚麻衣服，戴着木髓遮阳帽，他或者去中国人家里，或者去印刷室，或者布道、上课，或者与同行恳切交谈和制订计划。

有几次，父亲和其他人到内地去旅行，一走就是几天。通常是两个人结伴旅行，工作确定后，当地的长者会陪同他们。凡是有可能，他们更愿意坐船旅行，因为差会有一艘配了桨的帆船，可以用在这些旅行中。行程较长时，要求准备床上用品、食物和药品，以及成箱的书籍和传单。书籍和传单拟分发给已建立中心的成员，或给感兴趣的慕道友。

父亲回来时，全家人都很高兴；大人们热切地恳谈，我们这些孩子还太小，不能理解很深，除了从他们说话的声调里听出来，在这些当地人中间传教时收获的或大或小的喜悦与希望，还有失望。当地人中有许多人父亲以前从未见过，还有人从未听说过父亲等人在这些旅行中带给他们的新生活方式。对父亲的说教，有些人沉思、显示出兴趣却又犹豫不定，而另一些人则摇着头立马转身离开，这是常有的事。

【女子教育】

父亲每天给一个班的男人上课，他们预备成为传教士和教师，有时在他们自己的本土教会当牧师^①。在那很久以前的日子里，当地教堂和同工寥寥无几，这个时候主要是打基础阶段。母亲也教一个妇女班，经常和学生见面。

只是我不知道她们的身份。当然，在早期的这个阶段，不期望妇女们参加礼拜，或者成为活动在姐妹之间的"圣经妇女"。当时的清帝国还没有女子学校，因为男人断定说：女人不会学习，她们没有足够的脑力去学习，为她们开办学校是愚蠢的。我的印

too young to comprehend further than to gather from tone of voice, the various degrees of joy and hope, or disappointment, in their mission to these natives, many of whom they had never seen before, or who had never heard a word of the New Way of Life they had carried to them on these trips, which some received thoughtfully and with questioning interest, and others quickly turned from, with a shake of the head—as is always the case.

[Women's Education]

Father had a class of men he taught daily, who were preparing to become preachers and teachers themselves, and pastors over their own native churches, sometime. In that long ago day, there were very few native churches or helpers: it was mainly a time of laying foundations. Mother, too, had a class of women with whom she often met.

Just their status, I do not know. Of course they were not expected to take part in services, or to be "Bible women", going out among their sisters, at this early time. There were no schools for girls in the Empire then, since their judges—the men—declared women could not learn; they did not have brain power enough to do that; and to have schools for them was foolishness. My impression is that mother did try to teach a few women to read. They could commit to memory, more or less; that I know, for I can hear them singing, even now, in their meetings with her. Still, the echo carries, "Song tay chong cho te kop pwea", to the tune of "Watchman, tell us of the night". I realize a native might readily declare this is no language of his; but—as near as six or less years of age has it stored away in memory's cells,—and so quoted, with apologies!

There were other hymns translated into their own language which were in a book of hymns for their use. Among those translated, also they repeated simple verses, and the Lord's Prayer.

These were the embryo, however, of the future days of faith and education, when they all would be formed into a National Church, as we know is being done in this, our day. Father's petition and hope to the Reformed Church, was like seed sown to bear fruit after many days, in this process.

Late in our life in China, the new church was completed, very near the home of Mr. Talmage, and we children looked down from their upper verandah upon the building, from the foundation work up to

象是，母亲确实教过几个女人识字，她们多少能记住一些，这我是知道的，因为直到现在我耳边还回响起她们在与母亲会面时唱的歌，和着《更夫请问夜如何》②的曲调唱着"宋泰冲尖角码头"③。我知道当地人可能会轻易地说这不是他的母语，但这首歌在我接近或不到六岁的时候，就储存在记忆细胞里了，所以，上面这句歌词引用过来就成这个样子，抱歉了！

还有其他赞美诗被翻译成汉语，收录在一本圣诗书中供他们使用。在译作之中，他们也重译了简单的短诗和《主祷文》。

然而，这些都是明日信仰和教育的雏形，到那时所有这些将会形成一个全国性教会，正如我们看见我们的时代正在做的那样。在这一进程中，父亲给归正教会提出的恳求和希望，就像播下的种子，经过许久孕育出果实。

我们在中国生活的后期，新教堂建成了，距离打马字先生家很近。④我们孩子们就从他家楼上阳台俯视着这个建筑，从打地基开始，一直到建成完工。接着，献堂庆典的日子定了下来，引来大量的中国朋友和信徒，男男女女以及好奇的旁观者。我们两个家庭的孩子们也参加了典礼。干净的白墙、家具和甜美的气味仍留在我的脑海里，还有女人的叽喳声和婴儿的哭叫声，以及孩子母亲试图哄孩子安静下来的声音，所有这一切都发生在仪式进行中！但关于礼拜，我们年幼无知，没记住什么。

打马字先生和父亲温暖的情谊源自他们是那个年代在厦门最年长的传教士，有很多共同兴趣。乘同一艘船来华也使他们关系密切。后来，母亲去世后，打马字家对我们家孩子们分予的慈爱和关照，让我们温暖在怀，永远铭记。

我们经常在打马字家住上或长或短的一段时间。一次，一位密克罗尼西亚人来他家，带来了在海中岛屿传教工作的消息。他还带来了面包果，是在那遥远海岸生长的一种奇异水果。

打马字太太把我们都叫到她身边，给了我们一块面包果，告诉我们它的食用价值，指出它奇特的外皮等等，然后说，我们可能再也见不到这种水果了，应该好好看看，这样才能记住它。我们期待着它很

the finished church. Then a day of dedication was set, which brought a large concourse of Chinese friends and believers, men and women, and curious onlookers. We children, from both families attended. The clean white walls and furnishing and sweet odors stay with me still, and also the chatter of women and crying of babies as their mothers tried to hush them—all going on during the services! But of the services we were too young to carry anything.

Mr. Talmage's and father's warm friendship grew out of being the oldest of the missionaries in Amoy in their day, and with many interests in common. Coming out on the same ship made one of the close ties. And later, the kind and loving sharing of the care of the Doty children after mother's death, is always to be remembered warmly.

We were often at their home for longer or shorter visits, and once a man from Micronesia came there and brought news of the mission work among the "Islands of the Sea". He also brought breadfruit, as a curious growth of that far off shore.

Mrs. Talmage called us all about her, and gave us a piece, and told us of its value as food, and pointed out its peculiar skin, and so forth; and said, probably we would never see this kind of fruit again, and should look well at it, so as to remember it. We anticipated a treat; but it did not appeal to us, or make us regret we would never see the like again! Nevertheless, now I have that bit of memory, which I would not have had, but for "auntie Talmsdge"'s impressing it upon us—of a product of a far off country.

⌈Rebuilding the "Morning Star"⌉

This episode from "Micronesia" brings another story. We were often told about the "Morning Star", a little vessel which plied between the many islands of this group, to serve the missionaries in one or another of them. Then came the account of its being wrecked; and that the Sunday School children of America were raising money to buy another boat to take its place. Charley and I were very grieved over this loss, having had stories told to us of boys and girls, natives, missing its help. We were asked if we would like to help get some money, too, which of course, we were full of interest to do.

We were fitted out with a contribution sheet, and father took us to the different offices of the Tea Merchants, and other foreign places, where we placed before them the sad fact, and need of another boat, and asked if they would help. They

美味，但结果并没有吸引我们，也没有因为再也见不到它而让我们后悔！然而，我现在还有一点零星记忆，要不是打马字阿姨向我们介绍一个遥远国度的特产，我是不会有这种记忆的。

【重建"晨星"号】

密克罗尼西亚的趣事勾起了另一个故事。我们经常听说"晨星"号，它是一艘往来于这群海中岛屿之间的小船，用来为一个又一个岛上的传教士服务的。接着就听说它失事的消息，于是，美国主日学校的孩子们正在筹集资金，购买另一艘船来代替它。查理和我对这一损失感到非常悲痛，因为我们听人说起过，男孩、女孩，还有当地人怀念"晨星"号的助益。有人问我们是否也想帮忙筹些钱，我们当然很感兴趣。

我们准备了一张捐款单，父亲带我们去了各个茶商的办公室，以及其他一些外国人住所，我们把"晨星"号失事的厄难讲给他们听，并说需要一条新船，问他们是否愿意帮忙。他们对我们的恳求和我们这些孩子表示了极大的兴趣，在捐款单上签字并捐款。等我们回家的时候，我们为新"晨星"号募集到了100美元。那份捐款文件我仍保留着！在一篇关于建造第二艘"晨星"号的记述中，故事里包含着我们的名字，这对于一个7岁、一个5岁的两个小孩来说，着实令人激动！

【信号山与邮船】

父亲的一个日常事务是接收船只信号，并不辞劳苦地做记录。船只进港信号是从港口远处的基站通过旗帜和彩球在旗杆上或升或降发出的，内行人懂得旗语的意义，并只能通过望远镜看到。

无论何时，只要有船或"勇士"号驶进我们的水域，消息在我们社区传播时，就会引起极大的兴奋。无论是美国人、英国人、荷兰人、法国人还是东印度人的船，所有船只都载有邮件，可能已经在途中数月了。各种各样的消息可能会出现在朋友面前——欢乐或悲伤，痛苦或安慰。于是巨大悬念笼罩

expressed great interest in our appeal, and towards us children, and signed the paper and made offerings, until, when it was time to return home we had received one hundred dollars for the new "Morning Star". That very contribution paper is still in my possession! And in an account written about the building of the second "Morning Star", this story is incorporated with our names—a thrilling thing to two small children, seven and five years old!

[Signal Hill; Mail Ships]

One daily service father gave his painstaking care to recording, was the receiving of signals of shipping through flags and colored balls, lowered and raised on a flagstaff, with known meanings to the initiated, from a station far out in the harbor, seen only through a spyglass.

Whenever a vessel or "Man of War" was turning into our waters, great excitement followed, as the news was broadcast in our community. Was it an American, British, Dutch, French, or East Indiaman? All carried mail, which may have been months en route. And news of all kinds might be coming forward to meet friends—of joy or sorrow, distress or comfort. So a deep suspense seemed to hover over all the company, some of whom would gather at our house, as the place where first information could be had, and also was situated nearest to the outer harbor. As the vessels approached, first, the masts just rising above the horizon could be sighted by the naked eye; then the sails and hulls; and by this time, the spyglasses could discern to what nationality the vessel belonged, and to what class of ship.

If the "Stars and Stripes" flew at the stern, O! The thrill to our American family! If the cross of St. George was there, our warmest friends were cheered; and all of the American Colony would be glad too, for our interests were closely entwined, and our mails often, too, found their way to us through the British ships.

Our American ships would bring the most direct letters to us, or boxes, or perhaps a friend— a missionary—to join forces with those who waited to welcome them. If a British boat, an English or Scotch friend and his wife might be returning again to China, after a visit to their homelands, or new faces to add to their colony and make friends with all.

[Quarantine: First Childhood Sorrow]

Trading vessels often went up and down the coast and dropped anchor, and officers came ashore, com-

着大家，有些人会聚集在我们家里，因为在这里可以最先得到消息，而且离外港最近。当船舶靠近时，用肉眼最先看见的是刚从地平线上升起的桅杆，然后是船帆和船体。到了这时，望远镜就能分辨出这艘船是什么国籍，属于什么级别了。

如果星条旗在船尾飘扬，哦！兴奋是属于我们美国家庭的！如果英格兰圣乔治十字旗⑤在那里，我们就为我们最好的朋友们欢呼，所有的美国人定居点也会很高兴，因为我们的利益紧密相连，我们的邮件也经常通过英国的船只带过来。

美国船会给我们带来直接邮寄的信件或者箱子，也可能会带来一个传教士朋友，加入那些夹道欢迎他们的传教士队伍中。如果是一艘英国船，可能是一位英格兰或苏格兰朋友带着妻子回国探亲后再次返回中国，或者是新面孔加入他们的群体并与大家交好。

【隔离检疫：童年的第一个悲伤】

商船经常沿着海岸边往来，抛锚停泊，军官们也会上岸来，有时还会来看望我们。

每一次，只要船一驶进我们的港口，锚链发出嘎嘎的响声，并随着一股巨大的水花抛进深水里，父亲和其他一些人就会乘着小船来到他们身边，应邀爬上绳梯表达欢迎。我猜想有某种隔离检疫，但我确信检疫不很严格，因为有一个商人，他的妻子和孩子与这位船长同行，回程时又来看我们，这个商人曾拜访过我们家，还不止一次去打马字先生家。我们很高兴地看到我们的小友可可·梅森。但可可在打马字家得了重病，次日发现是亚洲霍乱，几小时后她就死了。自始至终，我们这些小孩子为她的痛苦感到难过，想陪着她，大人们也没有阻止。还好，我们没人染上霍乱。这是我们孩子们的第一个悲伤。

【孩子戏】

随着我们年龄的增长，母亲教查理和我一些小诗和赞美诗，我们跟着她一起唱，《圣经》章节和故事也熟悉起来了。我们从伦敦公会那里得到了一个玻璃罩着的盒子，大约18英寸×15英寸的规格，里面装着

ing in to see us sometimes. In every case, as soon as the vessel had ridden into our harbor, and the anchor chains had rattled down, and with a mighty splash dropped into the deep, father and other men would be off in their rowboats to their sides, and on invitation, would climb up the rope ladder and give welcome. I expect there was some sort of quarantine, but it was quite lax, I am sure, for one trader on a return trip, whose wife and child accompanied the Captain, and who had visited us in our home and with the Talmages in theirs, on more than one trip, came again, and we were very pleased to see Coco Mason, our little friend. But she became violently ill at the Talmages' home; and the next day it proved to be Asiatic cholera, and she died in a few hours. All the time until near the end, we children, who were so sorry for her sufferings, and wanted to be with her, were not prevented! None of us contracted the disease, however. This was our first childish sorrow.

[Childhood Dramatics]

As we grew older, Charley and I were taught little poems and hymns which we sang with mother; and Bible verses and stories became familiar to us. We received from the "London Missionary Society" a case—under glass—about eighteen by fifteen inches, of colored pictures of Bible stories and scenes, from those of Adam and Eve, through the Life of Jesus Christ, so were well acquainted with them.

We liked to play some of them—the Prodigal Son, in which Charley was the old father and Sammy and I were the two sons. I, as the sinning one, asked my portion of goods from the father and went off to a far country—way to the end of our long verandah, which seemed very far sometimes—and, waiting there among the husks for a little, came slowly back, and was met by the father, with outstretched arms, and really wept in my distress, saying, "Father, I have sinned against Heaven and in thy sight", and received the welcome home. It did not take much following of facts to satisfy little children.

We dramatized the "Last Judgment". Charley was the Judge, perched on the high back of a rattan chair, from which, he declared in a deep voice, "Depart from me" or "Come ye blessed" to Sammy and me, and baby "Mousie" who came along with us, and either climbed up the big chair in answer to "Come ye blessed", or turned in misery away as we "departed" to the far corner of the verandah again, with a sense of guilty terror upon us!

We played the "Good Samaritan", and others. Sometimes the

《圣经》故事和场景的彩色图片，从亚当和夏娃的故事，直至耶稣基督的一生，我们都如数家珍。

我们喜欢扮演一些其中的人物——浪子回头⑥那种，查理扮演老父亲，萨米和我扮两个儿子。我扮演一个不肖子，从父亲那里要了自己的那份家产，就动身到一个遥远的国度去，我沿着我家有时似乎非常遥远的、长长的走廊一直走到尽头，在谷壳中间等了一会儿，再慢慢走回来，这时"父亲"张开双臂迎接，不肖子在痛苦中真的哭了，开口说："父亲，我得罪了天，又得罪了你。"回家时却受到欢迎。不需要演绎太多的故事就能使小孩子们满足。

我们还演了一出"最后的审判"。查理扮法官，坐在高背的藤椅上，他用低沉的声音说"离开我"，或对萨米和我说"祝福你们"。尚是婴孩的小妹莫西和我们一起玩，听到查理说"祝福你们"，她就爬上大椅子，或者当我们带着一种负罪的恐惧，"离开"到阳台的远角时，她也痛苦地转身离开。

我们也演"好心的撒玛利亚人"⑦，还

有其他的角色。有时打马字家的孩子们和我们在一起，然后就有了拍打着翅膀、高兴地蹦来跳去的天使，努力回想歌词，唱道：

> 我变天使升仙，
>
> 众使并排而站；
>
> 额上皇冠璀璨，
>
> 手中竖琴轻弹。

还有：

> 天上神的宝座之前，
>
> 侍立孩童一万。
>
> 孩童罪责赦免，
>
> 化身圣洁欢快的乐团，
>
> 向我们至高的主啊，
>
> 致敬高歌，荣耀连连。

我猜想父母经常从某个隐蔽的地方偷看我们表演，但我不记得他俩因为我们对神的不敬而阻止我们。我们上演了《圣经》故事中庄严的一幕，也许是以上阿默高⑧耶稣罹难复活的方式演的。有一次，查理从高处摔了下来，断了一只胳膊，把我们吓坏了，但是他穿着母亲为应对这一紧急情况做的漂亮的小长袍几天后，一只袖管

Talmage children were with us, and then there were angels, who flapped their wings and skipped about in Joy, remembering and singing,—

> "I want to be an angel
> And with the angels stand;
> A crown upon ray forehead,
> A harp within my hand. "

and,

> "Around the throne of God in Heaven,
> Ten thousand children stand.
> Children, whose sins are all forgiven,
> A holy, happy band,
> Singing glory, glory, glory
> To our Lord Most High."

I expect that father and mother were often peeping at us from some hidden spot, but I never remember we were stopped, as irreverent. It was a solemn acting out of the stories, Oberammergau way, perhaps. Once Charley fell from his height, and we were frightened over a broken arm, but after a few days of wearing a pretty little wrapper which mother had made for such emergencies, with a sleeve hanging armless, like a hero, it was quite compensating!

My turn came next to wear it. Charley was cutting the string of a covered basket of oranges or tangerine, and I leaned over his shoulder at just the angle to catch the upstroke of his knife in my forehead, close up to the hair line (where the scar still can be felt). Terror over the blood that flew, and screams which brought both parents, and the bandaging and comforting that went on, is very vivid still, and also the lying down on the sofa with the pretty wrapper on as being quite satisfactory! This same little garment is still kept in a trunk which came from Amoy, with clothing—for "auld lang syne".

[Eating Mangoes]

A picture of mother comes to mind in connection with mangoes, which were brought in. We loved them, and eagerly laid hands upon them, but were stopped by her, as she quickly laid aside some occupation and said, "Don't touch them until I can cover you all up".

We were enveloped in a sheet or large towel, and told not to get up from our seats until all was eaten and Boa had brought water and washed our faces back to the ears, and hands and arms, 'most too roughly! Those of you who know

空空垂着，像个英雄一样，这倒成了对查理的一种补偿！

下一个就轮到我穿长袍了。查理正在砍断一筐柑橘篮子上的绳子，我斜倚在哥哥的肩膀上，所处的角度刚好赶上他上扬砍刀，刀碰在我额头上，靠近发际线处（那里现在仍能感觉到伤疤存在）。流血让我感到恐怖，尖叫声引来了父母，随后缠绷带和安慰话记忆犹新，穿着长袍躺在沙发上令人感觉相当满意！这件小长袍还保存在从厦门带回的箱子里，以记着"昔日好时光"。

【吃杧果】

我脑海里浮现出一幅母亲与杧果有关的画面，杧果是人家送的。我们都喜爱杧果，急切地想抓起来吃，但被她拦住了，她快速地放下手头的活儿，说道："在我把你们都包起来之前，不要碰杧果。"

母亲用床单或大毛巾把我们裹起来，告诉我们直到吃完所有东西才能从座位上站起来，保姆拿来了水，把我们毛毛糙糙地从脸洗到耳朵、手和胳膊。如果你了解杜果，就会懂得这种做法的必要性，因为杜果汁液极其丰富，而且它深黄色的污渍很难去除。

我还想起一两幅与母亲互动的画面，可以表明她管孩子的方式，或者是与我打交道的方式。我想，要给像我这样可能5岁出头接近6岁的孩子留下持久的印象，一定需要母亲拥有个人特点。有一天，我发现母亲在浴室或浴缸室里，一头乌黑的长发披散着盖在头上和脸上，全是肥皂沫，在一个从没有专业洗头洗发的地方和时代，她正好好享受着香波洗发。但对我来说，这看起来太可怕了，以为母亲正受到伤害。当然，我的尖叫声把父亲引来英雄救美，他把我抱在怀里，而母亲则拨开盖住眼睛的头发，眯眼看向我，用笑容安慰我，很快一切又都恢复了。

另一幕在我的脑海中生动地浮现出来，我下面要讲述出来，以免给人留下我们出现的场合都是自然但不严肃的印象。母亲叫我去试穿她正在做的一件裙子，我抗议说它太紧，弄疼我了，我不要穿。但抗议归抗议，没用。衣服料子是白色的，

the fruit, appreciate the necessity for all this care, as it is extremely juicy, and of a deep yellow stain, difficult to remove.

One or two other pictures of contacts with mother, which reveal her ways of dealing with us—or of my shares of it—come to mind. I think it takes a personal touch upon little children to leave a lasting impression—probably I was five, approaching six. One day I found mother in the bath, or tub room, with her long, dark hair thrown over her head and face, all covered with soap lather, enjoying a good shampoo, given by herself, in a day and place where professionals were unknown. But to me, it was a deed terrible to behold, and my mother was being hurt! Of course, I screamed, which brought father to the rescue, who took me in his arms, while mother opened up the blinding hair and peeped through with a reassuring laugh, and soon all was well again.

Another scene comes vividly to mind, which I will relate, lest the impression is given that no natural occasions ever arose for severity. Mother called me to her to try on a dress she was making; I protested that it hurt so, and I didn't want to, but—came just the same. It was white material, cross barred, made with baby waist gathered into a belt with short puffed sleeves, and the material was really—or felt to me—stiff and scratchy. I cried and squirmed and did all the naughty things which many another little youngster has done, and will continue to do until time ends, I suppose; and my mother was cross with me and talked severely to me, and insisted on continuing her work, most hardheartedly! just as good mothers always should do to naughty little girls, and big ones, too, who sometimes behave just as badly—and be given plenary absolution for being cross!

Our parents were always interested in having us children see any sight of note, and one night they awoke us, and brought us to the verandah to see a ship on fire from stem to bow and topmast to water's edge—a thrilling sight.

〔Plans for American Education; Mother & Friend's Death〕

About this time, father and mother began to talk of going home to grandfather's house, a year before mother died. We children were full of eagerness, and Charley and I learned we older ones were to stay in America to receive our educations. We pored over our children's books, which had pictures in them of school houses and

带横格，细腰用一条带子束着，泡泡袖，这种料子是——或者我觉得是——真的又硬又粗糙。我大哭，不自在地扭来扭去，像许多别的小孩子那样撒泼，我想，我还会继续闹下去，直到闹不下去。我母亲对我很生气，训斥我，而且硬着心肠坚持把裙子做完。母亲的表现就像善良的妈妈们对顽皮的，有时表现得同样糟糕的小女孩和大女孩应该做的那样，母亲发脾气也应该因此得到完全的宽恕。

我们的父母总是乐于让我们小孩看到任何有意义的东西。有一天晚上，他们把我们叫醒，带到阳台上去看一艘着火的船，大火弥漫，从船头到船尾，从中桅到船舷，真是一幅惊心动魄的场面。

【回国上学计划；母亲和朋友之死】

大约就在这个时候，父母开始谈论回外祖父家的事，这是母亲去世前的那一年。我们这些孩子翘首以盼，我和查理得知我们这些年纪较大的孩子将留在美国接受教育。我们仔细阅读儿童书籍，书中有校舍和美国男孩、女孩的照片，对我们来说孩子们很美，他们戴帽子、穿外套，女孩或者留着长长的卷发（我留短发），或者戴着包头软帽，系在下巴上，还穿长及鞋面的灯笼裤；我们梦想着有一天我们会像他们一样。

而且，校舍上总是飘着美国国旗。

但传教工作节外生枝，我们的父母被要求多待一段时间，他们听从了命令，结果我们都知道后来的悲剧结局。

一位苏格兰传教士在母亲生命的后半段来到厦门，他是山大辟⑨先生，对我这个近六岁大的小女孩很是慈爱。他总是很宠我，我记得他教我一首带副歌的苏格兰语圣诗《哦，主是多么爱我们》，我经常和他一起唱，当然还有其他的赞美诗。有一次，他邀请我去他那里过夜，这是一件非常愉快的大事。给我穿的睡衣摆放在那，他帮我脱衣服，把我抱起来，放在他的大床上。床的上方从天花板的正中垂到地板上挂着一张蚊帐（就像我们所有的床都有的同样的防虫措施）。终于，他在我身边躺下来，一切都那么美！但这是热带地区炎热的夜晚，我翻来

American girls and boys, who were wonderful creatures to us, with their caps and coats, and girls with long curls (my hair was short), or with bonnets tied under their chins, and long pantalettes which came down to the tops of their shoes; and dreamed of the time when we would look like them!

And always there was "our" flag floating over the school houses.

But complications came in the missionary work, and our parents were urged to stay longer, which they did, with the end result we all know.

A loving attachment between one of the Scotch missionaries who came to Amoy during the latter part of mother's life, was that between the little girl nearly six, and Mr. Sandeman. He always made a great pet of me, and I remember his teaching me a Scotch hymn with the refrain, "O, How He loves", and he and I used to sing it together, with other hymns too. Once he invited me to spend the night with him, such a great event, and full of delight. My nighty was put up for me to take, and he undressed and put me in his big bed, covered with a netting hung from the center of the ceiling to the floor (as all of our beds were likewise protected from insects). In time, he took his place beside me, all so beautiful! But it was a tropical night, hot, and I rolled and tossed until he picked me up and carried me to the latticed verandah, with the window thrown open, where the full moon poured down upon us. Often this occasion and that brilliant moon, comes to mind, when I gaze at full moons.

He talked to me, but it seems to have made no impression, and I guess I curled up and went to sleep by his side, leaning up against him. Shortly after mother's death, he died of cholera, leaving quite a heartache with the little girl.

My Last Birthday with Mom

One of the events quite naturally impressing me very vividly, was my sixth birthday, September, 1857, and mother died the next February, '58—so it was the last in which she partook.

Mrs. Boyd invited me to spend the day with her, and on returning, I brought with me presents: a beautiful doll with wax face and long curls, and a white dress trimmed with pink silk fringe. Such a treasure! Besides this, there was a toy set of blue and white china dishes, and a grey and blue dress which came from England with the doll, all trimmed with ruffles to the waist, and ribbons on the shoulders. Alas for my six years! It was far too large, and beyond my age.

覆去睡不着，最后他把我抱起来，抱到花格阳台上，打开窗户，一轮圆月的清辉倾泻在我们身上。每当我凝视满月的时候，就会想起那一夜和那皎洁的月光。

他和我说着话，但说的内容似乎没有给我留下什么印象，我想我蜷着身子，靠着他睡着了。母亲去世后不久，山人辟先生死于霍乱，我的心都碎了。

我最后一个与母亲共度的生日

一件自然使我印象深刻的事是1857年9月我6岁生日，因为母亲于1858年2月去世，这是她最后一次参加生日聚会。

有一天，包义德太太邀请我去她那里做客，回家时我带回礼物：一个漂亮的洋娃娃——蜡制的脸和长长的卷发，还有一件镶着粉色丝边儿的白色连衣裙。多好的宝贝！除此之外，还有一套蓝白相间的瓷碟玩具，以及与洋娃娃一起从英国带来的灰蓝相间的裙子一件，腰部都饰有褶边，肩上还系着丝带。唉，我怎么才六岁！它太大了，超出了我的年龄。尽管如此，我

中国故事
——罗蕾女儿回忆厦门生活（1851—1859）

The China Story
—Recollections of a Little Girl's Life in Amoy. China (1851-1859)

还是高高兴兴地看着它，相信我很快就能长大而穿上它了。然而，直到我们回到美国，能穿的时刻也没到来，因为此时没人穿褶裥饰边了，它看起来有些格格不入。尽管如此，我还是乞求得到它，感觉非常棒！我带着可爱的礼物回家，但好日子还没有结束。那位苏格兰女士——赛姆太太给我送来一个上乘的紫檀木针线盒，镶嵌珍珠母作为装饰，里面全是中国雕刻的象牙缝纫工具和其他物品，盒子内垫是粉红色缎子；还有一个抽屉，拉出来就构成一张文具齐全的写字台。我仍然把它摆放在我房间里，虽然它昔日的光鲜亮丽大多已逝，但可作为一段见证。

　　我曾经问父母亲我是否可以举办一个生日聚会，邀请我各行业的绅士朋友参加，再无他人。他们寄来正式的复函，说他们很乐意来，并请我或父母替我接受他们家跑腿男孩或仆人随信带来的礼物。（在我的宝贝中我还珍藏着一些复函。）一个人给了我一整块蓝灰色格子的丝绸，我去曼荷莲学院⑩上学时，料子做成了裙子。另一个人还给我一些银圆，他管它叫赏钱⑪，可

Still, I looked with great joy at it, and belief that I would soon be old enough to wear it! However, that time never came until we were in America, and it looked pretty queer, when at that time, no one wore ruffles. Still, I begged for it, feeling very grand! My day was not over on returning with the lovely gifts. Mrs. Syme, the Scotch lady, had sent me a choice work box of rose-wood, with inlaid mother of pearl decorations, and all full of Chinese carved ivory sewing implements and other articles, cushioned on pink satin cases to hold them; and a drawer when pulled out revealed a completely equipped writing desk. I still keep it in my room, in evidence, though its physical glories have to a great degree, vanished!

I had asked if I could have a party, consisting of my various gentlemen friends and no one else! They sent formal notes, saying they would be happy to come and asked me, or father or mother for me, to accept the accompanying presents which their "boys", or servants, brought with the notes. (Some of these notes I still have among my treasures.) One gave me a whole piece of silk, blue and grey plaid, for a dress, which was made for me when I went to Mount Holyoke. Another, silver dollars—"cumshaw" as he called it—asking to have it applied as best desired for me. There was a case of Chinese Puzzles of carved ivory. There were many of them, but most of them have met the fate of children's vandalism, though a few remain more or less intact.

There was a feather fan, decorated with Chinese painted flowers and birds and butterflies, and ivory carvings made the framework. A lacquered jewel case in fine workmanship came, and it is in good condition because mother rescued it from being appropriated to dolls' uses, with the plea that I would lend it to her for her bits of precious ware. I felt very magnanimous and proud to be granting it to her, and she transferred her treasures to the box, while I looked on and watched her make a silk pad for them to rest on. They were always kept there through mother's life, and since her death the box has never found other use, though the treasures have been scattered in various ways.

There were other gifts, I am sure, but they have not recorded themselves. My party, aside from the beautiful gifts, leaves in my mind a happy occasion with these young English and Scotch gentlemen, very attentive to me with stories and games to my liking, and some good natured bantering over our respective countries, which always seemed a satisfying thing

以如我所愿花掉它。有一盒象牙雕刻的中国谜语。还有许多，但大多数都遭到了被孩子们糟蹋的命运，尽管有几个多少仍是完好无损。

收到的礼物中还有一把羽毛扇，上面绘着中国画的花、鸟和蝴蝶，象牙雕刻做的扇骨。还有一个做工精细的漆器首饰盒。它现在的状况很好，因为母亲恳求我把它借给她，用来放一些珍贵的东西，使它免于沦为娃娃私用的玩具。我自觉很宽宏大量，也很自豪地把盒子给了母亲，她把她的珠宝都搬到盒子里去了，而我则在一旁看着她做了一个丝绸内垫。母亲在世时，一直用这个盒子放珠宝，她去世后，盒子再也没有挪作他用，但是那些珠宝或东或西地散落着。

我确信还有其他的礼物，但它们没有记录下来。我的生日聚会上，除了漂亮的礼物，在我的脑海里留下快乐的时刻是与这些年轻的英格兰和苏格兰绅士们在一起的时光。他们众星捧月，给我讲故事，做我喜欢的游戏，还有一些针对我们各自国家的善意逗趣，这种事似乎总是令人满意，因为我总是能临场发挥，应付裕如——我们管这叫"常规剧目"——这也是此刻大家希望的结果！

唉！在这样一个激动人心的生日过后，自然地，第二天早上，母亲发现我发烧了，必须细心照料，用凉水擦洗，一直吃了几天清淡饮食。状况好转后，我又满意地穿上了小长袍，最让我难忘的是，母亲给我送来方面包和番石榴果冻，面包片都放在一个漂亮盘子的边缘，中间有一堆果冻，然后喂给我吃。哦！太开心了——真是太美好了！这是和她亲密接触的最后记忆之一，因为她几个月后就去世了，其他的活动都没有这么亲近。

我们所有人共同享有的一份亲近肯定是来自父母双方的——每天早上我们穿衣前都要吃面包和红糖，而父亲则喝一杯咖啡缓解哮喘。我们吃着面包和红糖，他喝着咖啡时，我还记得他沉重的呼吸声和哮鸣音。然后老保姆帮我们穿衣服，我们下楼去吃早饭。年轻保姆的儿子做核桃雕，需要的时候会在桌边候着我们。

我一直在翻看厦门朋友们的照片，看

to do, because I always rose to the occasion—"bit", as we say—which was the end desired!

Well! After such an exciting birthday, quite naturally, the next morning mother found I was sick with quite a fever, and had to be petted and bathed off in cool water, and kept on a light diet for several days. When better, I again donned the little wrapper with satisfaction; and, best memory of all, mother brought me squares of bread and guava jelly lumps, on each piece, arranged around the edge of a pretty plate, with a mound of jelly in the center, and fed them to me. O! Such a delight—it was so good! This is among the last memories of her in a personal way, for she died a few months later, and other deeds are not so personal.

One thing which all of us shared must have originated with both parents—bread and brown sugar served to us before we were dressed, every morning, while father had his cup of coffee as a bracer against asthma, whose heavy breathing and wheezing I remember, while we ate the bread and sugar and he drank his coffee. Then old Boa helped us dress, and we went down to breakfast. The son of the young boa, who carved nuts, waited on the table for us, when required

I have been looking over photos of friends in Amoy, and seeing the face of Mrs. Lea, of the London Mission, brings to mind that she taught me how to crochet, and form a pair of baby socks of grey and canary yellow soft wool. This was probably during my fifth or sixth year, and mother was still with us..

Soft wools came only from England at this time. Yarns for use in knitting or weaving was what practical young America needed, and made with her spinning wheels, after sheep wools had been sheared and washed and corded at the farmers' homes.

An English person whom I do not remember, learning of my new interest in crocheting, gave me a quantity of beautiful colored soft worsteds, preserved in a zinc can, against moths and worms. I was fascinated with them, and pulled them about recklessly, snarling them up after the first enthusiasm.

We had a young Chinese friend who supported herself embroidering with silks and wools. These latter were very precious and hard to obtain—China is the home of lovely silks, we know, but not of wools—so mother, very sensibly, appealed to me for her work, and how much it would mean to her in earning her living, if I would give her these. My heart was touched, and I gladly did so, and felt rewarded, as even a little girl could see how grateful she was.

到伦敦公会李太太的面庞，让我想起她教我钩针编织法，我用灰色和淡黄色的软羊毛线钩织了一双婴儿袜。这大概是在我五六岁的时候，母亲还在我们身边。

这个时候，软羊毛只会来自英国。编织、纺织用的纱线是动手能力强的年轻美国人急需的，羊毛在英国农民家里剪下、清洗、绞成绳，再由李太太用纺轮纺成纱线。

有一个英格兰人，我忘记了名字，听说我新近对钩针编织产生了兴趣，就给了我一大堆颜色鲜艳、柔软的精纺毛线，保存在一个锌罐里防飞蛾和虫蛀。我被它们迷住了，不顾一切地把它们拉来甩去，一阵热忱之后，就把毛线缠成一团。

我们有一个年轻的中国朋友，她以丝绸和毛线刺绣为营生。我们知道，中国是美丽的丝绸之乡，但不是毛线之乡，毛线很珍贵，很难得。因此，母亲很理智，向我请求说，为了她的工作，如果我能把这些东西给她，这对她生计的意义很重大。我被感动了，也很高兴地同意了，因为就连我这个小女孩都能看出母亲是多么地感激，感觉得其所哉。

送王船 ⑫

我清楚地记得一个壮观场面，它最后一两次经过我们家时的情景。一年一度，中国大船、小船排成一列，浩荡地从厦门湾的某处出发，挂着风帆或划桨驶过我们的房子，远远驶离我们的视线，向他们的神明献祭求得抚慰，祈求来年获得神明保佑。船队由一艘崭新的小舢板打头，称之为"王船"，油漆闪亮，雕花彩绘，色彩斑斓，船上人员穿着节日盛装，船上显眼处飘扬着环形装饰。船只或乘风破浪，或摇橹划桨，每艘船上都有船员和彩旗，敲锣打鼓，击钹吹笙，一听就让我们联想起熟悉的中国音乐。所有船只都朝海上的某个地方驶去，在那里漂亮的"王船"将被烧掉，作为敬海神的额外祭品。每年，当我们看到"送王船"，我们的心都被深深地触动，但那只可爱的小船却一去不返！

Annual Spectacle: Sacrifice-offering to Sea-god

One spectacle I remember distinctly, the last time or two that it passed our house. It came annually, a Pageant of Chinese ships and boats, which started up the Bay somewhere, and sailed, or were rowed past our house, and far out beyond our sight, as a propitiation offered to their gods to, secure protection and help from them during the coming year. The procession was led by a new, small junk, beautifully finished, in carvings and paintings in many bright colors, carrying a crew in gala attire, and with rings flying from every vantage point. They sailed, or rowed by, each with its crew and flags, with gongs, and drums and cymbals and reeds, such as we associate with their known music. All went out seaward somewhere, and there the beautiful little junk was burned, as an additional offering to their god. Our hearts were much touched as we saw, annually, this spectacle, and the dear little boat going out—but never coming back!

【缠　足】

中华民国颁布了禁止缠足的法律，让

[Footbinding]

We have all rejoiced over the promulgation in

the Chinese Republic, of the Law against further foot binding; the distresses of which I caught sight of once, when wandering into old boa's rooms.

Young Boa had a daughter who came occasionally to see her, and have her bound feet redressed; the unbinding of the long worn bandages, and bathing of poor distorted feet where sores had developed, and then the distressing binding up again, with moans and sobs from the young girl, and beating from the mother as she shrank away from her, I looked upon.

This custom has not entirely been done away with, in the interior; but was the universal care that was given all young girls and women of good standing, with the same pitiful distresses, for generations.

Embroidering beautiful flowers and figures on "uppers" was one of the accomplishments of Chinese ladies, younger or older, and then making up the shoes, even stitching many layers of linen together into soles to support the uppers. I used to watch young boa make tiny shoes in this way for her child, and even attempted to make for my doll the same; but evidently owed to myself it was too much to do; the many folds of linen were so hard to push a needle through, up and down, and the silks tangled up so!

我们欢欣鼓舞。有一次，我逛进老保姆的房间时，看到了缠足的痛苦。

年轻的保姆有个女儿，偶尔来看她，她顺便把女儿的脚重新裹一下。解开长长的磨损了的裹脚布，洗洗生了疮、严重畸形的脚，然后伴着小女孩的呻吟和啜泣，再痛苦地裹上脚。女孩儿躲闪时，她母亲还打了她。我旁观了这一切。

缠足风俗在内地并没有完全废除，却引起了世人对所有年轻女孩和家境富裕妇女的普遍关注，一代又一代妇女遭受过同样悲惨的苦痛。

无论年龄长幼，给鞋帮绣上漂亮的花朵和图案是中国妇女的四德之一——女功，然后再缝制鞋子，甚至还把多层亚麻布纳成鞋底。我常常看到年轻保姆用这种方法给她的孩子做小鞋子，我甚至试着给我的玩具娃娃做同样的鞋子。但很显然，归于我自己的原因，我做不来；那么多层的亚麻布硬得连一根针都插不进去，没法穿针引线，就连绣花线也缠在一起了。

【注释】

① 本书涉及的神职人员称谓较多，此处有必要做一厘清。Pastor：(基督教教堂中的)本堂牧师，尤指在非圣公会教堂教区内有职位的。Preacher：布道者、讲道者，尤指以公开传教为职业的人。Minister：神职人员的统称——"牧师"，尤指长老会和不信奉英国国教教会的牧师；自16世纪以降，加尔文宗等新教教派反对使用priest(祭祀、神甫、牧师)或clergyman(牧师、神职人员)，而首先用minister指称牧师，现在主要用于持新教观点的低教会派(Low Church)，尤其是有教区职位的牧师。Missionary：(尤指在国外传播基督教的)传教士。在本书中，比较归纳起来，pastor有相对固定的传道、证道场所与信众；preacher，固定性相对稍弱，有时需要走街串巷去布道，在基督教入华的早期，在华南地区通常是男性传道者，教会如果聘用女性传道者则称之为Biblewoman；missionary是受教会委派到海外的传教士，作者的父亲罗啻属于这一类人；helper指牧师或布道者的助手。——译者注

②《更夫请问夜如何》，破晓歌，也称问星歌，美国作曲家洛厄尔·梅森(Lowell Mason，1792—1872)创作的赞美诗，是宗教题材。破晓歌在诗歌内容上常常出现对上帝的请求，在音乐上平稳的格里高利圣咏式进行，无不体现着宗教思想的影响，反映了世俗音乐与宗教音乐的交融。歌词第一句是："更夫请问夜如何？何故此星更向上？行人此行来预告，真理和平光福降……"——译者注

③"宋泰冲尖角码头"，是当地刚识字的妇女用发音不准的白话字音唱圣诗，本意想唱的似乎是"上帝创造天及地"，是现今《闽南圣诗300首(增订本)》的第一首。——译者注

④ 作者玛丽可能有记忆错误，她所生活的8年(从1851年9月16日出生至1859年10月离开厦门)，她懂事之后亲眼看到的，又在打马字家楼下附近的，厦门的教堂对不上号。新街礼拜堂建于1848年，献堂于1849年；竹树堂1850年，新竹树堂1904年；1863年三公会共建教堂竣工，时称"国际礼拜堂"，后更名为协和礼拜堂；三一堂则更晚，其主体建筑在1934年落成。——译者注

⑤ 现今英国国旗上的米字图案综合了原英格兰、苏格兰和北爱尔兰的旗

帜标志，这与英国历史有关。旗中带白边的红色正十字代表英格兰的守护神圣乔治（St. George），白色交叉十字代表苏格兰守护神圣安德鲁（St. Andrew），红色交叉十字代表爱尔兰守护神圣帕特里克（St. Patrick）。此旗产生于1801 年。——译者注

⑥ "浪子回头"是《新约圣经·路加福音》中记载的一个耶稣的比喻。一个父亲有两个儿子，小儿子要求父亲把归他的那一份家产给他，然后起身往远方去，在那里将分给他的财产挥霍一空，只能屈辱地以为人放猪为生。这时他决定回家，请求父亲的原谅。但是当他回家时，他的父亲在远处看见，就动了慈心，几乎不给他机会来表示悔改，就跑去抱着他的颈项，热切地亲了他，并宰了肥牛犊庆祝小儿子回来，又把上好的袍子给他穿，把戒指戴在他手上，把鞋穿在他脚上。大儿子听说后，对无耻的小儿子受到这样的优待，而自己一直忠诚却未受过奖赏，感到生气嫉妒。他父亲就出来劝他："孩子，你始终和我同在，我一切所有的都是你的。只是你这个兄弟是死而复活、失而又得的，所以我们理当欢喜快乐。"——译者注

⑦ "好心的撒玛利亚人"是基督教文化中一个著名成语和口头语，意为好心人、见义勇为者。源于《新约圣经·路加福音》中耶稣讲的寓言：一个犹太人被强盗打劫，受了重伤，躺在路边。有祭司和利未人（Levite）路过但不闻不问。唯有一个撒玛利亚人路过，不顾教派隔阂善意照应他，还自己出钱把犹太人送进旅店。耶稣时代，犹太人蔑视撒玛利亚人，认为他们是混血的异族人。耶稣用这个寓言说明，鉴别人的标准是人心而不是人的身份。犹太人自己的祭司和利未人虽然是神职人员但见死不救，仇敌却成了救命恩人。——译者注

⑧ 上阿默高，德国西南部巴伐利亚阿尔卑斯山区的一个村庄，傍依安珀河（Amper）流经的谷底，是极少数尚存的最著名的耶稣受难复活剧演出地点。在上阿默高，每10年就会上演一次《耶稣受难剧》，村里几乎过半的人都会参加演出，这在德国已广为人知。这个传统已经延续了几个世纪。相传17世纪时，整个欧洲面临着黑死病的传染威胁，上阿默高的居民也没有逃脱这个厄运。无奈之下，当地教堂的神父召集所有的村民到教堂祷告，祈求上帝的宽恕，并一起立下了一个誓言，每10年由全村人共同献演《耶稣受难剧》。自此以后摆脱黑死病，没有一个村民再因黑死病而死亡。上阿默高的村民信守对上帝的承诺，自1634年开始，每10年演出一次《耶稣受难剧》，到了1680年开始将演出年度改为每10年的"零年"。除极少例外，从未间断。现今的上阿默高，每座房子的墙壁上都画着色彩鲜明的壁画。这些画在墙上的

壁画叫作湿壁画，即使过上两三百年都不会褪色，因为它采用的是一种特殊的工艺。作画前画师先在墙面上涂上灰泥，这种灰泥要事先在水中浸泡一年以上，接着趁灰泥还没有干的时候，迅速用矿物质的颜料绘画，颜料就会浸透进灰泥中，永远都不会褪色。整个小镇似乎就是一个美术馆，所到之处艺术品遍布。这些壁画小的约有2平方米，大的差不多占据了整面墙壁，主题包括《圣经》故事、民间传说、老少皆知的《格林童话》和美丽的花草等。小镇还随处可见精美的木雕艺术品。——译者注

⑨ 山大辟（David Sandeman，1826—1858），英国长老会传教士，出生于1826年8月23日，幼年时就比同年龄的孩子稳重一些，少年时代的他则以坚忍不拔、生活有规律、有强烈责任心而显得与众不同。1844年11月27日，他来到爱丁堡，开始在当地的独立教会学院修读各门课程，包括拉丁文、希腊文、自然哲学、高等数学以及一些难度稍低的科目。他跟随威廉·汉密尔顿（William Hamilton）爵士学习逻辑学，跟随迈克·杜格安（M. Dougall）教授学习道德哲学，跟随班纳曼博士（Dr. Bannerman）、詹姆斯·布坎南博士（Dr. James Buchanan），以及坎宁安（Cunningham）校长学习神学及其分支，同时他还跟随约翰·邓肯（John Duncan）学习希伯来语，且对与之同源的其他语言分支的学习有所进展。读书期间，山大辟曾两次到法国和瑞士做短暂考察。1855年1月11日，他被批准进行传教，其后的那个星期日，他在格拉斯哥安德斯顿的萨默维尔（Somerville）先生的教堂中完成了第一次布道。数日后，他被要求在距离格拉斯哥3英里远的希尔海德主持仪式。2月，在那里开始了他的牧师生涯。然而山大辟早在五六年前就已萌生到中国工作的念头，因此，1856年10月11日，山大辟从马赛港出发，途经马耳他和亚历山大港后，于21日至苏伊士，11月8日至加勒，18日到新加坡，12月1日抵达香港。6日，他从香港起程，途经汕头，最终于9日抵达厦门。然而，他在这里工作的时间很短，1858年8月31日，当他还在为未来积极准备的时候，却因染上霍乱而去世，他的遗体被葬在厦门浪鼓屿的传教士墓地中，坟墓序号17-(9)。——译者注

⑩ 曼荷莲学院，是美国一所著名的女子文理学院，源于成立于1838年的曼荷莲女子神学院，1888年改为学院。该学院位于马萨诸塞州的小镇南海德利，为美国"七姐妹"学院之一。在19世纪，美国的女性高等教育虽然刚起步，但其女子接受高等教育的潮流却一发不可收，女子学院也势如破竹地涌现出来。"七姐妹"（Seven Sisters），作为美国7所历史最悠久的著名女子学院的传统联盟，也应运而生。与之相对应的"八兄弟"大学，即著名的常春藤

联盟（Ivy League）。——译者注

⑪ Cumshaw，赏钱，小费。洋泾浜英语，源自厦门话"kamsia"，表示感激。——译者注

⑫ 送王船，又称"烧王船"，是闽台沿海一带民间盛行的一种敬奉海神的传统民俗活动，至今有数百年历史。民众通过祭海神、悼念海上遇难的英灵，祈求海上靖安、渔发利市、风调雨顺、国泰民安。"闽台送王船"这一民间习俗，于 2011 年被列为国家级非物质文化遗产。——译者注

第六章　归程
Chapter 6　Journey Back to America

【母亲去世】

1858年2月的一天早上，我们家里似乎气氛紧张，人们在来回奔忙。打马字太太也在，母亲躺在床上，不一会，有人告诉我们几个孩子——查理、塞缪尔和我以及两岁大的婴孩莫西，刚出生的小妹妹和母亲躺在床上，并把我们带过去。我们看到一个小脑袋依偎在母亲胸前，对我们孩子来说真是伟大的奇迹、巨大的喜悦。

然后我们被送到保姆那里。一两周后，有一天早上，我们正在闹腾，这时父亲出现了，脸上挂着悲伤，让我印象深刻。即使这个时候，当父亲来到我们跟前，用手指划过我们每个人的嘴唇，虽然一句话也没说，但我们懂得，我们要保持安静。后

[Mother's Death]

One morning in February, 1858, there seemed to be a tense atmosphere in our home, and people moving about. Mrs. Talmage was there, and mother in bed, and soon we—Charley, Sam and I with baby "Mousie", two years old—were told there was a new baby sister in bed with mother, and we were brought in to see the little head nestled on her breast, a very great wonder and delight to us children.

We were then sent out to the nurses. So for a week or two; then one morning, when we were quite noisy, father appeared and the sadness on his face impressed itself on me, even then, as he came to each one of us and laid a finger across our lips, with not a word said; but we understood we were to be quiet. Then later, my dear Mr. Sandeman lifted me up in his arms and carried me to the head of the bed on which mother lay; and I was told by him, that God was taking my mother to be in Heaven with him. And he held me in his arms until her breathing ceased, and comforted the little girl's sorrow in gentle ways. The agony on my father's face, I seem to remember plainly.

Then at once, a way to nourish the little baby had to be found. Old boa put warm milk in a blue and white teacup, with a piece of cotton soaked in it, one end of which was held by her finger to the mouth of the baby to suck. It seemed to succeed, and so the little wailing baby was fed until it died, a few months later.

Mother was beloved by the whole circle of foreigners—missionaries, merchants, and officers of American and British vessels—and all Chinese men and women with whom she came in contact. There was a large funeral. Some points I can recall. A long line of Chinese women came, in their mourning garb of white, filing in, to look on her face, with wailing and mourning.

There must have been a short service at our house, then we older children were led by someone (I dressed in black, with a cape and collar trimmed with crepe) out of the house and down on the wharf to a boat. There was a long procession of these loaned ships in the

来，我亲爱的山大辟牧师把我抱在怀里，走到母亲躺着的床头，他告诉我，上帝要带我母亲去天堂，与其同在。他把我抱在怀里，直到母亲呼吸停止，他用温柔的方式安慰我这个小女孩的悲伤。我似乎清楚地记得我父亲脸上的苦痛。

接下来，必须立马面对的问题是如何喂养新生婴儿。老保姆把温热的牛奶装进一个蓝白色的茶杯里，里面浸着一条棉花，她用手指捏着一端，放到婴儿嘴里让她吮吸。这个方法似乎成功了，所以这个啼哭的小婴儿一直这样喂养，直到几个月后（7月2日）夭折。

母亲深受整个外国人圈子——传教士、商人、美国和英国舰船上的军官，以及所有与她打过交道的中国人的喜爱。葬礼场面很壮观，我零零星星记得一些。穿着白色丧服的中国妇女排着长长队伍，鱼贯而入，瞻仰母亲的遗容，哀悼、痛哭。

在我们家里，一定是举行了一个简短的礼拜。然后，有人领着我们这些大一点的孩子们（我穿着黑色衣服，带有披肩，领口上镶着绉边）走出家门，下到码头，上了一条小船。在港口里，有一长列租借

来的船只，均配有水手。每艘船只上的美
国国旗皆降半旗，从船尾垂入水中，跟着
第一艘载着用国旗裹着的灵柩（当时还不
用骨灰盒）的船，送到鼓浪屿上的外国传
教士公墓。

到达码头时，所有船上的水手都举起
船桨并将其竖起，第一艘船上的美国水手
把仍然裹着美国国旗的灵柩抬起放在肩上，
然后朝墓地走去，所有人都紧随其后。母
亲被慈爱的双手放到墓穴里，打马字先生，
作为父亲最亲密的伙伴，一遍遍在母亲遗
体上方重复着那一句熟悉的话："复活在
主，生命在主。"

没娘的孩子有人管

我们在厦门一直待到1859年10月。在
母亲去世后的时间里，我们得到了友善的
传教士朋友们的精心照顾。在某些方面，
一个男人，一个忙于自己工作的男人，是
做不好的。但父亲是一个非比寻常的人，
能够在一定程度上担起责任，既当爸又当
妈，在家里他总是把我们聚在一起。

harbor and manned by sailors. Each
boat with an American flag at half
mast, trailing in the water from
the stern, followed the first boat
which carried the coffin (no caskets
in those days), wrapped in our flag,
over to Kolongsu Island, where the
Missionary Cemetery is located.

As we came to the Landing,
the sailors on all of the boats raised
their oars upright, while the American sailors in the first boat lifted
the coffin to their shoulders, still
wrapped in our flag, and walked, so,
to the Cemetery, all following closely behind. And mother was laid in
her grave by loving hands, and the
familiar "I am the Resurrection and
the Life", repeated over her body
by Mr. Talmage, very probably, as
father's closest associate.

Auntie Talmage, Mr. Rapaljo

We stayed in Amoy until
October, 1859. We
were cared for through all those
months after our mother died, by
kind friends among the missionaries, in ways a man, and a busy one
in his own work, could not well
do. But father was a very unusual
type of man, being able to assume
the cares, to a degree, of mother as
well as father, and he always kept us
together in our home.

We spent many days and hours with our kind friends, Mr. and Mrs. Talmage, whose four children grew up with us, and of nearly the same ages. "Auntie Talmage", as we called her, taught a little school for her children which we attended, as we had become old enough by now to begin studying. She kept an oversight of our clothes, too, with other loving hands to assist; as well as with a Chinese tailor, who used to work under mother's directions and patterns.

During this time, a young man, Mr. Rapalje, joined the mission; and I think he must have lived with us, as we saw him in so many intimate ways at all times. We children loved him; he was like an older brother, telling us stories and incidents of interest, and accompanying us on our jaunts and making, or mending toys, and aiding us in ways that mother used to care for us, at times. Only a few months ago, I saw the notice of his death, in his ninetieth year. He had been living only a few miles from our home, after retiring from his missionary work; and I did not know it, or I would have tried to renew our acquaintance.

Packing up

At last the time came when we constantly talked of

我们和我们的好朋友，打马字先生和太太一起度过了很多时光，他们的四个孩子和我们几乎是同龄人，一起长大。我们称打马字太太为打马字阿姨，她为自己的孩子开班授课，因为我们此时到了学龄，也跟着一起听课。打马字阿姨也负责我们的穿衣，加上其他关爱之人来帮忙，还有一位中国裁缝，过去常常在母亲指导下，效仿母亲的方式工作。

在这段时间里，一个名叫来坦履①的年轻人加入了布道工作。我想，他一定是和我们住在一起，因为我们不论什么时候总能看到他，往来密切。我们孩子们很爱他，他就像一个大哥哥，给我们讲故事和趣事，陪我们远足、制作玩具或修理玩具，有时用母亲过去照顾我们的方式帮助我们。就在几个月前，我看到了他去世的讣告，享年九十高龄。他从传教工作中退下来后，就住在离我们家仅几英里远的地方，而我却不知道，否则我早就设法去再续前缘了。

打点行囊

最后，我们常常谈到回美国的时间到

了。父亲一直在打包，收拾一箱箱的书，或者是小摆设，抑或其他物品。女士们为孩子们挤出时间，或者指导中国裁缝为我们三个月的漫长旅行做衣服，因为在航行中，船上缺乏淡水，我们没法儿洗衣服。

来坦履先生就像父亲有力的左膀右臂，抑或像他的大儿子一样，因为父亲的健康已很脆弱。

终于，离开的日子到了。"凯西"号快船在港口抛锚并开始卸货。这时，"凯西"号轻盈、高高地卧波海上，我们坐船绕着它看了一圈，它在接下来的三个月内成为我们的家。我——小玛丽，很容易被大炮或不同寻常的景象吓到，大闹了一场，恳求不要把我带到那艘船上。船太单薄了——就像一块竖立的木板——它肯定会翻倒！但是，我的恳求无人理睬，所有上船航行计划都有条不紊地推进时，我很不高兴；直到几天后，父亲又把我们带出去，船在水中沉得很低，使它看上去很宽阔，这让我很满意，我的麻烦算是过去了。

传教船向"凯西"号进发，大大小小的箱子，一件一件的行李，并没有家具，

going to America. Father was always packing boxes of books, or bric-a-brac, or other commodities; and the ladies saved for the children, or directed the Chinaman tailor in making clothing for the long three months' journey, in which we could have no laundry work done on account of lack of fresh water.

Mr. Rapaljo was like a strong arm for father, whose health had become frail, or was like an older son to him.

Finally the day arrived when the clipper ship "Kathay" dropped anchor in the Harbor and began unloading her cargo. At this time, when she was the lightest, and sat up high out of the water, we rode out and around her to see our home to be, for three months. Little Mary, so easily frightened at guns or unusual sights, made a great disturbance, begging not to be put on that ship; it was so thin—like a board set up on edge—and it would surely tip over! It caused me much unhappiness, when my implorings were unheeded, and all plans kept maturing to go on board of her for the voyage; until a later day, when father took us out again, and the ship sat so low in the water, as to make her satisfactorily broad; and my troubles were over.

The Mission boat carried out to the "Kathay", the boxes, large

and small, and pieces of baggage;
no furniture—that was disposed of
among our friends, until only the
bare necessities were left to go with
us. Our ship had changed her position in the Harbor to one farther
out—towards the open sea, to catch
better breezes and tides. There
were no other passengers on board.

The farewells were said to
many friends gathered at our home,
foreign and native ones, very heartfelt and sad ones to the elders, but
which did not carry much sorrow
to the children, in the midst of
keen interest in the new adventure
before us.

We all gathered on the deck
of the Mission boat, with a group
of friends accompanying us, and
started away to the "Kathay", in the
afternoon sun of early October. We
were not to set sail until sometime
in the night.

Soon we spied, far back towards the city, a speck on the water,
hardly distinguishable at first, but
growing clearer, it proved to be a
rowboat, with someone waving a
white cloth vigorously, and oars
flashing through the water; and we
all concluded someone was coming
to our vessel, and watered eagerly,
until a Chinese friend called, "The
children's kitties were left behind,
and we have brought them in this
bag." "Tommy" and "Tatty", our

这一切都交给我们的朋友们搬运，直到只剩下随身携带的最基本必需品留给我们携带。我们的船改变了它在港口的位置，更向外滩，靠近公海，以便更好地利用风向和潮汐扬帆起航。船上再没有其他乘客。

许多朋友聚拢在我们家告别，有外国人，也有本地人，对年长者而言，离别的话既真诚又伤感；但对孩子们来说，这并没有给他们带来太多的忧伤，因为我们对前面的新冒险充满了浓厚的兴趣。

一群朋友陪着我们一起聚在传教船的甲板上，在这十月初午后的阳光里，驶向"凯西"号。我们要到夜里才能升帆起航。

很快，我们发现，远远地在城市方向，水面上有一个小点，一开始很难分辨，但越来越清晰，结果是一艘小船，有人用力挥舞着白布，船桨在水面上快速划动。我们都得出结论，有人奋力划水，要到我们的船上来，直到一个中国朋友喊道："孩子们的小猫被落下了，我们用这个袋子送过来了。"汤米和泰缇，我们亲爱的小白猫！我们长辈们脸上带着惊恐的神色，也带着一丝愧疚。我们紧紧地抱着我们珍贵的宠物，嘴唇紧闭，那些话是不言自明的："我们永远不会放弃它们！"但是一只大狗跳了过来，后面跟着一只小猎犬，两只小猫后背上的毛发根根竖起，嘶嘶的猫叫和咆哮的犬吠传递出各自的意图，一场激战在即。接着，一名军官用恐怖的结局吓唬我们说，我们的宠物可能会被大狗撕成碎片，然后把小猫递给我们。两害相权取其轻，我们只好泪流满面地把猫咪交还给把它们带过来的中国好朋友，算作离别礼物，尽管事实上，父亲在我们离开前已经把它们送给了一个能照看好它们的人。当夜幕降临时，大家最后道别，传教船向港口转向离开，父亲带我们到铺位上，把我们塞进了被窝，睡了一整夜。第二天早上，当我们来到甲板上时，我们满眼是湛蓝的海水、白色的帽子，风帆猎猎，浪花划过我们的船头向后，在船尾翻腾，但是看不见陆地。这是我们大冒险中看到的第一幅新风景。我们立刻发现有很多事情让我们闲不下来。

dear white kittens! There was a look of consternation on the faces of our elders, and a bit of guiltiness, too! But we held our precious pets tightly, with set lips. Those unspoken words said, "We will never give them up!" But a huge dog came bounding along, followed by a terrier; and every hair on the kits' backs stood on end, while hisses and growls gave an accompaniment to their intentions, and a battle royal was imminent. So, egged on by harrowing tales from an officer, of the tearing to pieces of our pets, which were dealt out to us—as the least of two evils, we tearfully gave them back to the good friend who had brought them to us, as a parting gift. Although, in fact, they had been given away to one who would care kindly for them, by father, before we left! As darkness drew on, the last farewells were spoken, and the Mission boat turned its course about again towards the Harbor, and father took us down to our berths, and tucked us in for a long night's sleep. The next morning, when we came on deck, our eyes met the vivid blue water, and white caps, and sails bellowing out, and foam cutting our prow and seething from the stern, but no land! Our first new sight on the great adventure! We found many things to busy us, at once.

Seasickness

The first experience was when father called us down to the cabin for morning prayers. We felt so full of life and eagerness, under the new aspects of water, and ship, in motion—so different from the quiet rippling, waters of our rowboat trips, and the furled or flapping sails in the Harbor—that we begged to wait a little! Alas! Prayers were hardly spoken, before we began to feel queer, and a little resentful, too, thinking if we could have stayed up on deck, we wouldn't have had to get into our berths for a week of seasickness!

The other children were over it first, and I was carried up, and laid on a mattress, on the deck, to let the pure salt air work its healing. Every detail of these first days, was deeply impressed on my mind. I wore a red dress, plaided with orange threads, quite Chinese, with little red buttons which looked like carnelian, down the front; and was lying there quite limp and forlorn, when a great comber dashed over the deck, drenching me and floating me about on the receding wave, not near enough to the side of the ship to make danger of being washed overboard, however! I became entirely well from the seasickness

晕　船

第一番经历是父亲叫我们到船舱做晨祷。这与以前我们划小船旅行，清漪粼粼，在港口内帆卷帆舒完全不同，这里是水急浪高、大船乘风破浪的新景象，我们感觉充满了活力和渴望，我们请求再稍等一会儿。唉！祷告几乎还没说出口，我们就开始略感不适，也有一点怨恨，心想如果我们能在甲板上待着，就不用在我们的铺位上晕船一个星期了。

其他孩子们先登上甲板，我被抬上来，放在一个床垫上，让纯净的海风发挥它的疗效。海上航行最初日子的每一个细节都给我留下了深刻印象。我穿了一件红色连衣裙，用橘黄色的线编成彩格图案，很有中国味，裙子有一些红色的小纽扣，看起来像红玛瑙，垂在前面。我无力地躺在甲板上，孤苦伶仃，这时一个大浪冲过甲板，打湿了我，回浪冲得我四处浮动，但是离船舷还有距离，没有被冲到船外落水的风险。这次经历之后，我的晕船就完全好了!

船上宠物梦

　　尽管艄楼甲板禁止进入,我们在甲板上漫步时还是发现了许多东西。有一个大笼子,大约三英尺高,用来装鸡,摆在一个装满小猪的围栏上方。当小猪把鼻子和前蹄放到栏杆上,吱吱叫时,看到粉红色的猪鼻子总是令我们很开心;同时鸡把头和脖子从板条之间伸出来,咯咯地叫着、吵着。还有一个围栏装满大鹅,非常凶恶地对我们发出嘎嘎声示威,对它们,我们似乎从来也提不起兴趣。从船头到船尾,还有一群猴子。那只大纽芬兰犬,与我们形成了一种彼此难割难舍、你侬我侬的温暖情谊。但是,我们似乎从来没有和那只小猎犬有任何瓜葛。

　　查理、塞缪尔和我刚满十岁、六岁和八岁,年纪够大了,可以一起做事情了。当莫西没有紧紧依偎在父亲身旁和父亲说话时,她就和我们一起跑来闹去。因为她是婴孩,跟父亲很亲近,父亲也很亲她。她经常管父亲叫"牧师",说话前总是说:

after this experience!

Dream of Pets

We discovered many things as we roamed over the deck, though were not allowed on the forecastle. There was a large cage, about three feet high, for chickens, placed over a pen full of little pigs, whose pink noses always amused us, as they put them and front feet on the railing, and squealed, while the chickens thrust their heads and necks out between the slats, and cackled or scolded, at the same time. There was a pen of geese, which never seemed to interest us—they hissed at us so viciously. And there were monkeys "fore and aft", and the great Newfoundland dog, for which we formed a warm attachment, which he returned towards us all. The little terrier we never seemed to have anything to do with.

　　Charley, Sam and I were old enough to do things together, just ten, six and eight. "Mousie" trotted about with us, when she wasn't snuggled down close to her father, talking away to him, for she was the baby, and very close to him, and he to her. She often called him "Dominie", prefacing conversation with "Well, dominie—". We used to hear the ministers greet each other by that name, and she took it up!

One day we asked a Mate if he would sell us a chicken, which we could keep in our part of the ship for a pet. He said yes, for a very shiny Chinese penny, cash, with a square hole in the center of it—it must be that!—and also asked where could we keep it, out of its own cage?

We said, "We could keep it in one of the deep coils of rope which were about the deck." (and often in use.)

"Very well," he said.

O! The faith youngsters have, even if they are so foolish! We scoured and scoured the penny, and trailed it in the water over the stern by a string tied in the hole, but it came up no shinier, and we had to give up our pet chicken. Then the mate suggested if we could sprinkle salt on the tail of a seagull, of which many followed our ship, we could catch it, tame it and have it for a pet.

So, eagerly we started out on this trail. At times, when the ocean was rough, the bow of the ship rose high on the ascending crest of a wave, while the stern dipped low down, and we watched for the right conditions—the descending stern, and some gulls floating near to us, both at the same time—which

"好吧，牧师——"我们过去常听牧师们用这个称呼问候彼此，然后她就学会了。

有一天，我们问一个大副能否卖给我们一只鸡，我们可以把它当宠物养，放在船上我们的位置上。他说可以，但一定要一枚崭新闪亮的外圆内方的清朝铜钱不可，别无他法。大副还问我们，把鸡从笼子里拿出来之后我们放在哪里养。

我们说："我们可以把鸡放在甲板上某个深深的绳圈里。"（绳子常常被用到。）

"很好。"他说。

哦！这就是年轻人的信念，即使他们是如此荒谬！我们把这枚硬币擦了又擦，用一根绳子拴住方孔，在船尾后的海里拖着它走，但它没有变得更闪亮，所以我们不得不放弃购买宠物鸡。然后，大副建议，因为有许多海鸥跟在我们船后，如果我们能把盐撒在海鸥的尾巴上，我们就能抓住它，驯服它，再把它当宠物养。

于是，我们迫不及待地开始尝试。有时，当大海波涛汹涌的时候，升起的浪尖就会把船头高高推起，当船尾下沉的时候，我们就寻找恰当时机——下沉的船尾加上

中国故事
——罗嘉女儿回忆厦门生活（1851—1859）

The China Story
—Recollections of a Little Girl's Life in Amoy, China (1851-1859)

几只海鸥在同一时间靠近我们——机会不止一次地出现。我们曾经准备好了盐，但是，空手而归的伤悲并没有让孩子们的心情多么沉重，我们很快又高兴起来。

途 中

我们向南穿过巽他海峡，它处于爪哇岛和苏门答腊岛之间。岛上有青草、绿树和居民，变成了真正的居住之所，而不是我们在第一堂地理课上发现的枯燥名字。马达加斯加岛和我们所看到的海岸上的所有地方也一样，我们在这些地方靠岸抛锚。我还记得海岸边高高的绿色堤岸，小船云集在我们大船周围，载着货物——大部分是水果和蔬菜。有柚子（像葡萄柚），还有大蕉、香蕉、山药和杧果。

一些蔬菜和水果被储存起来，留着当没有新鲜蔬菜水果时再用。像杧果等一些易烂的水果，我们立刻吃掉了；然后按照我们通常处理脏衣服的方式，把我们染了黄色污渍的裙子和男孩子们的亚麻外套扔给了渔民们，因为母亲不在了，没有人把

recurred more than once. We were ever ready with the salt, but, alas! Another disappointment met us! But sorrows do not weigh heavily on children, and our happiness was soon restored.

en Route

We sailed down through the Straits of Sunda, between Java and Sumatra Islands, which became real places, with green grass and trees and people on them, instead of just names which we found in our first Geography lessons! And so with the Island of Madagascar (and all places on the coasts that we saw) where we cast anchor. I recall the high green banks of the shore, and boats swarming about us, with their wares—mostly fruit and vegetables. There were pumelos (like grapefruit), and plantains and bananas, yams and mangoes.

Some of these were stored away, to be dealt out later, when we had been longer away from any fresh fruits and vegetables. Some perishable, like mangoes, we ate at once; and then threw our yellow stained dresses, and linen coats of the boys, over to the fishers, according to the way we always had to do with our most soiled clothing.

There was no mother to wrap us up in sheets; and probably she would have followed the same course, as the only available one to do, if she had been with us!

Another incident comes to my mind, concerning mangoes. When we reached grandfather's house, in the early days when everything was new, someone spoke of mangoes for dinner; and I was delighted to find our favorite fruit grew in our new homeland; but when they were placed on the table, what appeared but green pepper sour pickles!!

The yams served us longer, and for two purposes: first, as a vegetable; they were not like the yams we know here, but of a grey color, and when prepared, somewhat of the texture of mashed potatoes, which we children liked. Then they served as one of the entertainments of our days. We liked to gather at the galley, to see the cook turn the fried yam, by tossing it up and catching it exactly in the right spot in the pan, only the other side up, showing the golden brown of the finished product! This was our delight, and the cause of a superior, triumphant look on the cook's face, as he always succeeded!

Our food was, as would be supposed, simple and wholesome; but with no meats (except corned,

我们裹在被单里。如果她和我们在一起，也许她会用同样的方法把我们裹起来，因为这是保持干净的唯一方法。

关于杧果的另一件事出现在我的脑海里。我们到达外祖父家之后，最初的日子一切都很新鲜，有人谈到了杧果晚餐；我高兴地发现，我们最喜欢的水果生长在我们的新家乡；但是，当杧果晚餐上桌的时候，却发现是酸青椒泡菜。

山药储存期更长，而且可以两用：首先，当作蔬菜。它不像我们在这里熟知的山药，竟是灰色的，加工后有点儿像土豆泥的口感，这是我们孩子们喜欢的。其次，它成了我们那段时间的娱乐项目之一。我们喜欢聚在厨房里，看着厨师把煎山药向上用力一抖，在空中再用煎锅妥妥地接住，山药就翻了个面，煎好的一面朝上，呈现出诱人的金黄色。这是我们喜闻乐见的事，厨师脸上也因此挂着一副胜人一筹、得意扬扬神色，因为他从不失手。

正如所想的那样，我们的食物简单而健康。但没有肉（除了腌制的，而且长时间浸泡在盐水桶里的咸肉，但味道可想而知！），在那些日子里，没有冰箱，船上也没有活牲畜，除了我们经常吃的家禽和猪。

我想起我们享受其中的煮熟的梅子布丁和黑糖蜜，还有在任何时候都有的那种又大又厚的海员硬饼干。

如果我们的食物是液体的，那就好玩了！随之而来的后果可能是这样的：当勺子还未到嘴边的时候，船突然摇晃一下，结果就洒到鼻子、眼睛或衣服前襟上！船尾颠簸一下，引起灾难性的后果是：碗或盘子都滑向桌子的另一边，或掉到地板上，碗里、盘里的东西随浪涛起伏，疯狂地泼来溅去。

可怕的是，我们孩子们每天喝三次红茶或咖啡。我经常纳闷为什么要喝这些东西——可能缺乏好的饮用水，也没有牛奶——当时浓缩奶或奶粉还是闻所未闻的。

船长的宠物猴

猴子给我们带来欢乐，也有恐惧。有只小猴是斯托达德船长的宠物。当它坐在他

and of long standing in casks of brine, with suggestive consequences!). There were no refrigerators in those days, or live stock on board, other than the fowls and pigs, from which we were often served.

Boiled plum duff comes to mind and black molasses, in which we reveled! There were the big, thick, sea biscuit, at any and all times.

If our food was liquid—alas! Alas! Such consequences may have followed! A lurch of the ship at the moment when a spoon was half way to the mouth, caused a landing in nose or eye, or down the front of clothing! And a lurch back of the boat, ended in disaster, with bowl or plate shunting to the other side of the table, or on the floor, and the contents madly splashing back and forth at the will of the waves!

Dreadful to say, we children drank black tea or coffee, three times a day! I often wonder why—probably lack of good drinking water, and no milk—condensed or powdered not known then.

Captain's Pet Monkey

Monkeys were our delight, and terror, too. One little fellow was a pet of Captain Stoddard. Often his tiny fingers ran through his hair, as he sat on his shoulder, delighted if it found a delicious morsel! It was often given lumps of sugar by him.

One day little monkey was quietly enjoying his treat, within range of my arms. Quite wickedly, I pinched its cheek, protruding with a lump, with results I did not anticipate, for he flew at me in a great rage, and bit my side through the thin clothes I wore, leaving a scar which my morning bath can reveal to this day, if I cast my eye in that direction—a daily reminder of a long ago experience. Screams brought a crowd about me, ready to enjoy any diversion in their monotonous lives, whose grinning faces seemed to say, "She got what was coming to her!", if put into modern parlance.

Sailor and Stewardess

I had a pet sailor, Sebastian, who made or repaired sails. His bunk was a cubbyhole full of sails and materials, on which he curled up for his night's sleep. I used to watch him spread out the sails on the deck, and match patches to put over rents, and then see him put the palm over his thumb and push, in and out, the big needle and cord he sewed with, while telling

的肩膀上时，它小小的手指常常从前往后给他梳头发，如果发现了点儿美味食物，它就会很高兴。船长经常给它喂些方糖。

一天，小猴在我怀里静静地享受着美味。我恶作剧地捏住它的脸颊，揪起一个肉团，结果没料到它勃然大怒向我扑来，咬穿了我身上薄薄的衣服，在我身体一侧留下疤痕。时至今日，我晨浴时，如果把目光投向那个方向，还能看到疤痕。它每天都在提醒我很久以前的那段经历。我的尖叫声引来一大群人围着我，在单调的航行生活中，人们随时准备碰到乐子消遣一下，他们咧嘴而笑的脸上，用现代的说法，似乎写着："她罪有应得！"

水手与乘务员

有一个水手，我非常喜欢，叫塞巴斯蒂安，他制作或修理帆船。他的床铺是一个装满帆布和材料的小窝，晚上蜷曲在上面睡觉。我过去常常看着他在甲板上摊开帆，用零头布料把裂缝补上，然后看他把手掌放在拇指上，把他缝的大针和绳子穿来穿去，同时告诉我海上的故事。

　　我们在船上还有另一个好朋友——女乘务员，安。她总能随时满足我们五花八门的需求，甚至帮助我缝补衣服，在漫长的人生中，我一生酷爱缝纫就是早年那些日子里培养起来的。我在船上给布娃娃做衣服，虽不够好，但有安的帮助，勉强凑合。我想要做一顶帽子，向她要些布料，她给了我一块红黑斑点相间的印花棉布。我用硬纸剪了一个圆儿做头部的顶部，把棉布缝上去，又把它连到一个直条上，做成环绕的帽带，然后剪一个中空的圆形做帽子边沿，缝到帽带上，这样就有帽冠、帽带、边沿，完全是一顶令人满意的帽子了。我相信，我感受到了一个创作者或发明家的兴奋！那顶红黑相间的印花布小帽子对我来说弥足珍贵，我抚摸着它，欣赏着它的奇妙。

　　然后我喜悦的翅膀折翼了，我跌落到失望之地；因为帽子对洋娃娃的头来说太小了，根本没法戴。此时此地吸取的经验教训，使我终身受益。那就是：一个人在行动前，应该先量度好；当一个人脱离实际时，事实基础才是最宝贵的。

me sea yarns!

We had another kind friend on board—the stewardess, Ann, who always fitted into needs of many kinds, at all hours, even helping me try to sew; for the passion of my long life was developing in those early days. I made doll clothes on the ship—such as they were—but assisted by Ann, they answered the purpose. I attempted a hat, asking her for material, and was given a bit of red and black dotted calico or print. I cut a round of stiff paper for the top of the crown, and sewed the calico on, and joined it to a straight piece for the band around; then cut a shape with a hole in the middle, for the rim, which was sewed on to the band—altogether quite a satisfactory hat, with crown, band and rim; and I felt the thrill of a creator or inventor, I do believe! The little red and black calico hat was precious to me, as I caressed it and viewed its wonders!

Then my wings were clipped, and I came down to earth with disappointment; for it was too small for my dolly's head and never could be worn! A lesson was learned then and there, which has stood me in good stead throughout my life. One should take measurements before undertakings; and when one's head is among the clouds, a foundation in facts is most valuable.

Sailing North

The next sight of land on our long voyage was the Light House on Cape of Good Hope, and a strip of gleaming white sandy beach, which father called our attention to, with the surf rolling up and breaking over it, as ever it does; and then talked to us about Africa, and this sight which we might never see again, but which would be interesting to remember.

One night, as our ship was turning towards northern waters, father called us together again, and pointed out the Southern Cross, telling us to note the four brilliant stars which formed its head and foot and arms, so we would well remember this too, for that would never appear in our sky of the Northern Hemisphere. We had often seen the cross while in our Amoy home, but this talk fixed it clearly in our minds.

One day while in the Southern waters, there was a shout, "Whales ahead." One big fellow was spouting water, and soon we were riding through a school of them, which we could plainly see, close to the side of our ship, many of them together. They were not ferocious, and apparently eager to get away

由南向北

在我们漫长的航行中，再一次看到的陆地是好望角的灯塔，以及一条长长且闪闪发亮的白色沙滩，父亲喊我们来看岸边浪涛翻卷，击碎在沙滩上，一如既往；然后给我们讲解非洲，此时的风景我们可能再也见不到了，但这是值得记住的。

一天晚上，我们的船转向北部水域，父亲再次把我们召集在一起，指着南十字星座 ②，告诉我们注意观察那四颗明亮的星星，它们形成了十字星座的头、脚和双臂，所以我们也会牢牢地记住这个，因为它永远不会出现在北半球的天空。我们过去经常在厦门的家中看到北十字星座，但这次谈话把南十字星座清晰地印在我们脑海里。

航行在南部海域时的某一天，有人大喊："前边有鲸鱼！"一个大家伙在喷水，很快我们就穿过一个鲸鱼群，可以清楚地看到，挨着我们的船边，许多条鲸鱼在一起。它们并不凶猛，显然反而急切地想离开我们，很快就游走了。

有一次，水手们成就感满满，他们用一块咸肉做诱饵，用一个大鱼钩钓上一条鲨鱼。鲨鱼一定是饿坏了，因为它急切地跃起想抓住咸肉，结果被拉到前甲板上，它狂暴地翻腾着，直到精疲力竭。

我们途中只遇到过一艘船，还发了信号，但没有收到有价值的信息，这让斯托达德船长和父亲都感到失望。

父亲帮助斯托达德船长用象限仪测量，并每天记录航海日志，所以在人生要确定好方向的哲理开始教给我们之前，我们早就不断地有实例来注解：

　　　大风吹，船儿行，

　　　一船西，一船东，

　　　风不变，道不同，

　　　非风劲，帆之功。

有一天，一艘失事船的残骸——一块舱口盖、一根船柱、一截桅杆和其他残骸，漂浮在水面上。我们满怀敬畏，因为我们知道一些可怜的水手和乘客已经沉没。

我们遇到了一场大风暴。孩子们被关在舱下一两天，禁闭空间的污秽气味久而

from us, and soon passed on.

The sailors had great sport once, catching a shark on a large hook, baited with a piece of salt pork. He must have been hungry, for he sprang for it eagerly, and was brought aboard on the forecastle deck, and thrashed around in great fury until exhausted.

We passed a ship only once, and signals were given; but no valuable information was gathered, to the disappointment of Captain Stoddard and father.

Father helped Captain Stoddard with the Quadrant, and keeping the daily log; so we had continued illustration, long before lessons from Life began, that,

"One ship drives east; and one drives west,
By the selfsame wind that blows;
'Tis the set of the sails, and not the gales,
That tells which way we go."

One day parts of a wreck floated by—a piece of hatching, a spar, part of the mast, and other debris. We felt awed, as we knew some poor sailors and passengers had gone down.

We encountered one great storm. The children were kept down below for a day or two, and the foul odors of that imprison-ment still remain. Finally, towards evening, we were allowed to come up on deck to see great waves rising and falling, and breaking over the decks, and deep blue sky and dark water; all ominous to us, though known to our elders to be vanishing clouds instead of gathering ones.

A little bird was driven against a low sail. Father caught it, and the poor little creature was so exhaust-ed, it made no resistance. We put it in a box, and took the best care of it that we knew how, with warm bits of cloth to cover it and something to eat and drink, all of which was untouched as we constantly peeped at it as it lay as if nearly dead. We were filled with high hopes of keep-ing it always as a pet, if it lived. But the next morning, on opening the box and peering under the covers, the bird lifted its wings and dashed off—as we watched it as long as it could be seen—probably to its own destruction still, as no land was near. It had been blown by high winds out of its course near some shore. So we lost our third pet!

As long as we were in the warm zones, I had my daily tub from the broad ocean, for if "Ma-homet couldn't go to the mountain, the mountain could come to Ma-homet". Sailors drew buckets (gut-ta-percha ones, instead of wood

不散。最后，临近傍晚，我们被允许上到甲板上，看到巨浪翻腾，拍打甲板，天空深蓝，海水黝黑。对我们来说，这一切都是不祥之兆，尽管我们的长辈知道，乌云即将消散，而不是聚拢起来。

一只小鸟被风雨吹落在低帆上，父亲抓住了它，这个可怜的小家伙已经筋疲力尽，没有挣扎。我们把它放在一个盒子里，用我们所知最好的方法精心照料它：用暖和的布片盖住它，给它吃的和喝的，但所有的东西都没有动过，我们不停地偷看它，它躺在那儿，几乎像死了一样。我们充满了希望，如果它能活下来，就永远把它当作宠物来养。但是第二天早上，当我们打开盒子，从布片往下看的时候，小鸟一振翅倏地飞走了。我们一直看着它，直到看不见为止。因为附近没有陆地，它很可能飞向自我毁灭。它原本是被近岸强风吹得偏离了路线才上了我们的船。所以，我们失去了第三只宠物。

只要航行在温暖的水域，我就每天洗海水浴，从广阔的海洋里取水，因为"我不向山行，山必走来迎"③。水手们用水桶（杜仲胶做的，不是木头或金属的）从海里提水上来，把满桶水倒在我头上，而我就裹着睡衣，站在一个鲜艳的红色浴盆里，同时父亲总是站在旁边，忠诚地守护着我。其他孩子们不喜欢倾盆而下的海水，因此都被"赦免"了。

赤道无风带

当我们到达大西洋时，我们进入了赤道无风带。当我初次读到柯尔律治《古舟子咏》④时，诗歌的一部分似乎是"亲历重现"，生动而真实，因为我们也静止不动，"就像一幅画中的航船，停在一幅画中的海面"。正如我们几天来看到的那样，大海就像镜子般明亮、平静，到处都漂浮着五颜六色的水母，船帆无力地耷拉着，酷热难耐，太阳几乎晃瞎人眼。

然后，某一天，一股急流冲击着镜子般的大海，船帆躁动起来。在后桅顶上垂头丧气的星条旗扬起了头。那命令的声音召唤水手们扬帆起航。水手们爬上护桅索，随即传来了"是！是！"的回应声。很快，我们就从停泊的地方启动向前，波纹在船舷两侧荡开，越来越快，我们又一次出

or metal) full of water and poured them over my head, as I stood in a bright red tub, in my nightie, my father always standing by me in faithful guardianship! The other children did not relish the downpour of salt water, and were excused.

The Doldrums

As we came up the Atlantic, we reached the Doldrums. When I first read "The Ancient Mariner", a part of it seemed like a "twice told tale", vivid and true, for we, too were "as idle as a painted ship upon a painted ocean". As we saw it for days, the sea was like glass, with rainbow-hued jellyfish floating everywhere, and sails hanging limp, while the heat was intense, and the sun almost blinding.

Then a day came when a riffle struck the glassy sea, and the sails stirred restlessly. "Old Glory" lifted its head, after hanging so dejectedly from the mizzen peak. The commanding Voice called to man the sails, and the "Aye, aye" came promptly, as the sailors climbed the shrouds. Soon we were moving off from our camping spot, with ripples hitting the sides of the ship with increasing rapidity, and we were speeding away again.

As we neared the Equator,

father called his children to him, saying, "We are going to cross the Equator soon, and if you will look through the spyglass, you will see the straight line across it."

We gazed in wonder and awe, and there it was, plainly to be seen! The mates stood around with twinkling eyes and twitching lips!

At last, Pussie's wits worked, and she exclaimed, "We can't see the Equator! Now I know why you took one of my hairs yesterday. You wouldn't tell me then!" And we shouted in glee that we had caught him.

Land Ahead

At last we came to the cold days in the North Temperate Zone. It was January. I do not remember any sensation of it, until we reached the shore. Father put woolen underwear on us, which we said "pricked", however. It must have been a mild winter, for it is easy to recall scenes of ships docking, laden with ice hanging from masts and sails, or covered with snow.

Then one morning early, the Captain called down to our cabins, "Land ahead!"

We rushed up on deck, and looked and looked, but saw noth-

发了。

当我们接近赤道的时候，父亲把孩子们叫到身边，说："我们很快就要通过赤道了，如果你们用小型望远镜看一下，你就会看到横穿赤道而过的那条直线。"

我们惊奇而又敬畏地凝视着镜头，那条直线就在那儿，显而易见！伙伴们站在那里，目光闪烁，嘴唇哆嗦着！

最后，我灵光一闪，大声说："我们看不见赤道！我现在知道你昨天为什么拿走我的一根头发了。你当时不跟我讲！"把父亲的诡计戳穿了，我们高兴得大叫。

前方有陆地

最后，我们迎来了北温带的寒冷日子。这是一月的冬天，我记不得是什么感觉了，直到我们到了岸边，父亲把羊毛内衣给我们穿上，然而我们都抱怨毛衣扎人。那一定是个暖冬，因为现在很容易想起船只靠港的场景，桅杆和帆上挂满了冰，或盖着雪。

然后某天清早，船长向我们的船舱喊道："前方有陆地！"

我们冲到甲板上，看了又看，但什么

也没看见，这时父亲指着远方的地平线，告诉我们那黑线不是水面上升起的云，而是陆地！是美国！

看着看着，黑线条越来越清晰，越来越高。从那以后，我们的时间都花在看新风景了。我们觉得这片土地非常多沙，不像我们一路见过的青草绿树的海岸。后来，靠得更近些，陆地看起来就像是被一片片白糖覆盖了！但父亲说，那不是白糖，而是冰和雪，在遥远的厦门我们在故事里读到过但从未亲眼见过的！

然后，检疫官出现了。我记得当时我很困惑，我为什么要在这些人面前脱衣服，直到最终似乎让他们满意了。

我们的船仍在向伊斯特河⑤上的码头缓慢前进。我们不要忘记，快速行驶的蒸汽船今天随处可见，但当时并非今天所看到的通用轮船。

水面上的景象映入眼帘，我们还看到了河岸上的房子。还有在狭窄水道两岸的大堡垒，炮口对着我们，怒目而视。

最后，我们靠岸了，锚链哗啦啦的声

ing, until father pointed to the far horizon and said that dark line out there was not a cloud rising over the water, but Land! And it was America!

As we watched, the line grew plainer and higher. Our time from then on was occupied in seeing new sights. We thought the land was very sandy—not like the coasts we had seen, with grass and green trees. Later, when closer to it, it looked as if it were covered with patches of sugar! But father said no, it was snow and ice, which we had read about in our stories, in way off Amoy, but which we had never seen!

Then the Quarantine Officers appeared. I remember being puzzled as to why I should have to undress before these men, and finally seem to please them!

Our ship was still making its slow way up toward the dock on the East River. Steamers with their fast motion were not the universal ships which are seen today, we must remember.

Such sights as met our eyes on the water, and such houses on its banks! And the great forts on either side of "the Narrows", with guns glaring out at us!

Finally we came to land, and the clatter of anchor chains roared again. Friends came at once on board to greet father and "the children"; not our very own ones—they were too far away to make the trip to New York City on the uncertainties as to when we would arrive, with no telephones and few telegraphs, or any wireless, to announce that we had been sighted off shore. But what curious sights greeted us from our dock—so many carts drawn by horses, new to us. Specially fascinating to us were the little houses drawn by them too—something like the sedans we had been accustomed to, only these had horses in front, instead of coolies in front and back. There were no coolies to be seen anywhere, or Chinese men of other ranks—not a single one!

Father was busy meeting friends and customs officials, and with overseeing the unloading of our baggage and boxes from the freight holds, but he stopped to tell us that these little houses were carriages, and that we would go in one of them soon! It was hard then to possess our souls in patience!

At last we bid good bye to Captain Stoddard and one or two favorite sailors and Ann, and our home for three months, and descended the ladder down to "terra firma", which reversed the order and gave us unsteady "land legs", instead of sea ones; and found ourselves in one of the wonderful little

音再次响起。朋友们马上登船来迎接父亲和孩子们；但不是我们自己的朋友——他们离得太远了，来不了纽约，因为我们什么时候抵达无法确定，即使在岸上已经能够看见我们的船了，也没有电话、电报或无线信号来通知他们。但是，在码头上我们看到的新奇景象是那么多马车，很新鲜。特别吸引我们的是马拉的小房子，就像我们熟悉的轿子，只不过前面拉车的是马，而不是前后抬轿子的苦力。到处都看不到苦力，也没有其他阶层的中国人——一个也没有！

父亲忙着与朋友们和海关官员会面，并监督从货舱中卸下行李和箱子，但他还是停下来告诉我们，这些马拉小房子是马车，我们马上就会坐上一辆。此刻，我们按捺不住激动的心情。

最后，我们告别斯托达德船长，一两个最要好的水手、乘务员安，以及我们住了三个月的"家"，沿梯而下，踏到坚实的大地上，但是乾坤颠倒，我们在海上不晕船，现在却立足不稳，"晕陆地"⑥。然后，我们就置身于一个美妙的小房子里，沿着码头小跑起来，到了街上。我们在一家小商店停了下来，父亲把我们都带进去，戴上了围巾和连指手套，这对我们来说是另一个奇迹——我们的手、脖子和耳朵都被盖住了！

回　家

我们遇到的下一个惊喜是，当我们离开马车的时候，父亲说："我们现在要过河，去新泽西州。"

我们静静地坐在一间阴暗、闷热的房间里，有几扇高高的窗户，看不到窗外景色，完全不同于今日装着大大低窗的精美船只，能把河流上下游景色一览无遗。我们正纳闷什么时候上船并划到对岸，这时得知已经过了河，我们彻底困惑了！那是父亲唯一一次没有意识到我们四个无知的小家伙的疑问，既没有看见船，也没有船夫，也没有一艘大帆船，仅仅是静静地坐在黑屋里，就过河了！哦，好吧。有许多更深层次的思考在他心中激荡，也有许多

houses, jogging along the wharf and into the street. We stopped at a little store, and father took us all in, to be fitted to scarfs and mittens, which were other wonders to us— our hands and necks and ears to be covered!

Going Home

The next surprise we met was when we left the carriage and father said, "We are going to cross the River now, over to New Jersey.

We sat very still in a stuffy, dark room, with bits of windows high up, out of which we could not look—far different from the fine boats and large low windows which command the view up and down the river, of the present day—and wondered when we were to get into a boat and be rowed over; and were altogether puzzled to learn that we had crossed it already! That was once that father did not sense that the four little ignoramuses could not understand how we crossed, with no boat or boatmen in evidence, nor a large sail-boat either,— just sitting still in a dusky room and getting there! Ah well! He had many deeper thoughts stirring his heart, and questions to ask himself, and to answer; and sad memories were beginning to meet him, as old reminders crowded about him, and thrust themselves upon his sight.

In those days, railroad travel was very primitive, and trains few and far between, and no stations nearer to grandfather's house than Newark or Morristown. So father's inquiries as to when we could get to Morristown, brought the information that nothing but a freight train would be going for hours, though the conductor said we could ride in the caboose of this one if we wished, which we did. It was our first experience in seeing a railroad train, or riding on one, add very exciting it seemed to us, and satisfactory, too, to be really riding on one, a mode of travel which we had only seen in pictures!

At Morristown, we were told Hiram Smith's four horse or mule milk wagon (full of milk cans) was at the station, and we saw it—grandfather's big wagon, full of milk!

We took a hack and started out on the seven miles' ride to Troy, to the Homestead. We had warm coats made of woolen material and lined with flannel, with long sleeves and skirts—the boys' much like the girls'—but underneath, our girls' dresses were low-necked and short-sleeved, and we possessed nothing else but clothes provided for tropical conditions. We were

问题自问自答；睹物思人，往事涌现，历历在目，悲伤的记忆开始向他袭来，百感交集。

在那时，坐火车旅行还很原始，车次少之又少，离外祖父家最近的车站是纽瓦克或莫里斯敦。因此，父亲问询车站我们什么时候能到莫里斯敦，得到的信息是只有一列货车，要开好几个小时。售票员说，如果愿意的话，我们可以坐这列货车车尾的乘务车厢。于是我们就上去了。这是我们第一次看到并乘坐火车，让我们感到非常兴奋，也很满意，因为这种旅行方式我们只在照片上看到过，现在真的坐在火车上了！

在莫里斯敦，有人告诉我们，外祖父海勒姆·史密斯的四匹马或四匹骡子拉的奶罐车（装满牛奶罐）在车站。于是，我们看到了——外祖父的四轮大马车，装满了牛奶！

我们乘坐一辆出租马车动身回家——七英里路程之外的特洛伊城。我们的保暖外套是羊毛材料做的，长袖，内衬法兰绒，穿短裙；男孩们穿得大同小异，但是我们女孩里面穿的是低领、短袖连衣裙，除了热带天气的衣服什么也没有。很明显，我们如此充满兴奋和惊奇，以致于隆冬时节，天近傍晚，我们都没有感到寒冷，直到我们开始说"我们的脚冻麻了，啊"。我们一下子冻透了，路程却只走了不到一半，马车里的毯子几乎不保暖。因此父亲说："孩子们，把腿盘起来，把脚坐在身下。"据我回忆，这种做法似乎很令人满意，我们暖和起来了，令人称奇，因为我们看过的男孩们溜冰照片所展示的就是这样取暖的。

我判断大约四点钟，在一个漆黑的、阴沉的冬夜，我们停在外祖父母家的前大门，我们太小还感受不到伤感，不过是把它当成我们亲爱的母亲的家。

在当时，乡下没有电报，只知道有人看到"凯西"号。家人们知道不久以后，父亲和埃莉诺的孩子就会到来。外祖母是第一个欢迎我们的人，在房门前迎接我们，她一声没发，却饱含千言万语，然后我们穿过门厅，走进客厅，外祖父在那里迎接我们。我还是个孩子，对这一路的静默感到寒意和敬畏，但随着年龄增长，我意识到这次见面是一场巨大的考验，往事像潮水一样涌上外祖

so full of excitement and wonder that, apparently, we did not feel the cold of a rather late afternoon in January, until we began to say "our feet pinched us. Ah!" The cold had struck, and we were only about half way there; and very little protection in the hack's blankets. So father said, "Sit on your feet, children; curl them up under you", which, as I recall, seemed entirely satisfactory, or we were warm—filled with thrills; for this was what made nice, which our pictures of boys skating had shown!

About four o'clock, I judge, of a dark, cloudy winter evening, we drew up to the front gate of our grandparents' home, too young to feel sentiment further than that it was our dear mother's home, also.

In those days, with no telegraph accommodations out into the country, it was only known that the "Kathay" had been sighted, and the family knew that some day soon, father and "Eleanor's children", would arrive. Grandmother's welcome was the first for us, as we were met at the front door, given in silence too full for utterance, and then we went through "the hall" into the sitting room, where grandfather's greeting came. As a little child, I felt the chill and awe of all this silence, but with later years, I realized the great ordeal it was, and the flood of memories which rushed over the grandparents and over father—of the last time father had stood in the same room, but with the beloved daughter by his side, just leaving for the great and terrible adventure; and now the return without her, but these four little ones—Eleanor's children—in her place. Soon aunt Marcia came in. She was a child about ten years of age when they went away; now, a mother of two children, one born three weeks before our arrival (and she was at her father's house for a time)—baby Kellie, whom I took to my heart then and there, and used to rock and sing to her, whenever opportunity offered.

When we saw aunt Marcia, we older children were filled with awe and wonder, and did not speak to her, but clung to father's arms and coat and whispered, "Is she mother?" I thought mother had gone to Heaven—the likeness was so strong to our childish minds!

At once there had to be arrangements made for us. The rooms had been prepared and waiting for days, but it was January, and an open fire should be built, and the room warmed, before we could go upstairs; and our little girls' dresses were made for tropical weather—low-necked and short-sleeved!

父母和父亲的心头：上次父亲站在这一间屋子里，而他们心爱的女儿就站在父亲身边，即将启程踏上那伟大而恐怖的冒险之旅；但现在父亲回来了，而他们的女儿却没回来，在女儿曾经站着的地方却换成了四个小家伙——她的孩子们。不久，马西娅姨妈进来了。父母离开时，姨妈还只是个十岁左右的孩子，现在已然是两个孩子的母亲了，最小的一个是在我们到达前三个星期（她在她父亲家住了一段时间）刚出生的小凯莉，当即我就喜欢上了小凯莉。此后，一有机会，我就轻摇着凯莉，唱歌给她听。

当我们看到马西娅姨妈的时候，我们大点儿的孩子都充满了敬畏和惊奇，没有和她说话，而是紧紧地抱着父亲的胳膊和外套，低声问："她是妈妈吗？"我以为母亲已经去了天堂，可姨妈长得太像她了，给我们带来的冲击如此强烈！

我们亟须安顿好。房间几天前就已经准备好了，但三九寒天，在我们上楼休息之前，壁炉要生火，房间要烧暖，我们小女孩的衣服还是为热带天气而制作的——低领、短袖！

【只吃米饭！】

我们年纪大些的孩子吃得惯晚餐的食物，但小莫西坚持要米饭。无论是某个善良的天使布置下去为那顿餐饭准备米饭，还是我们等到米饭做好再开饭，或者是莫西饿得受不了被迫垫补一点面包和牛奶充饥，我仍然清楚地记得，她总是提出"只吃米饭，别的不要"，而且一天三顿。在家里，或者在别人家的饭桌上，米饭不可或缺渐成共识，这一情况持续了很多天。

次日早上，头等大事似乎是准备布料给我们做高领长袖的围裙衣（男孩们总是被裹得严严实实！）。

我主动提出要缝制那些衣服，当然没啥问题，但是缝纫似乎是我唯一的技能，或许有人说起我在这方面干得不错。外祖父问我是否有顶针，我可没有。这也问得太令人奇怪了！我想。接着他说："我们必须到附近的一家小商店买一个。"而那里也应该卖些方格花布。他和我牵着手走到那

[Rice—Nothing Else!]

We older children accommodated ourselves to the food offered for supper, but little "Mousie" insisted on rice. Whether some good angel had directed rice to be prepared for that meal, or whether we waited until some could be cooked, or whether a coming appetite forced a compromise on bread and milk, it remains a clear recollection that she always asked for "rice, nothing else", three times a day! At home, or at someone else's table, it grew to be recognized as an imperative necessity, for many days!

The very next morning, the first thing of importance seemed to be to get material to make high-necked and long-sleeved aprons for us (boys always were covered!).

I offered to sew on them, very maturely, to be sure, but sewing seemed to be my only accomplishment, and perhaps a little bird had told of some of my efficiency in that line. Grandfather asked if I had a thimble, which I did not have, quite remarkably, I think! And he said, "We must go to a little store near by and buy one"; and also some gingham should be provided there too. So hand in hand, he and

I walked over there, on the hard, frozen ground, which seemed very rough to my feet; while my eyes looked out on big patches of snow—the first snow storm was still before us, mantling the whole countryside in white.

Then an apron was cut, and in time I was given a hem to do, feeling very grown up, to be sewing with my grandmother and others, rushing the covering of those bare arms, which I have no recollection of ever feeling cold, however—so much so that grandmother remarked we must retain, still, some of the tropical heat in our veins!

Aunt Mary

I do not have a clear idea of when we first met aunt Mary. She was away at boarding school, in Montclair, when we arrived, but soon came home to see us.

Grandmother's health began to show the long strain of cares she had borne with her own large family and household responsibilities, and it became evident that she could not meet the new burdens alone. But devotion to the beloved daughter made a decision positive, that the children must stay in "Eleanor's home", and be cared for by them. Who, then, was to take the large share of the

儿。路面上结着冰，非常坚硬，我的脚走得很辛苦。当我的眼睛望着大片大片的积雪时，第一场暴风雪仍在我们面前，白色的大雪覆盖着整个乡间。

然后，有人裁剪了一条围裙衣，最后让我包边儿。和外祖母还有其他人一起做针线活，给裸露的胳膊快速缝制袖子，让我觉得自己长大了。尽管裸露着胳膊，我不记得感觉多冷，以至于外祖母惊叹说，我们的血管里一定还保留着一些热带的高温！

小姨妈

我记不大清楚我们第一次见到玛丽姨妈是什么时候。当我们抵达时，她离家在蒙特克莱尔，读寄宿学校，但很快就回家来看我们了。

由于外祖母长期以来承担着照顾一大家人和操持家务的重任，过度劳累对她健康的损害开始显现，她显然无法独自应对我们带来的新负担。但对爱女的挚爱让她做出一个明确的决定，孩子们必须留在埃莉诺的家，并由他们照顾。那么，肩负起大部分责任的人除了小姨妈还能有谁呢？一个青春少女，还在上寄宿学校，自此以后，如果不是永久，至少也要暂时辍学在家，而她仅仅十六七岁！想想今天无忧无虑的同龄女孩们，能否一力担起如此重负？常言道，"你的日子如何，你的力量也必如何"，此话不虚，因为有这些分外之责压在她身上。

她以极大的勇气迎挑起重担，她值得信赖、能干，是忠诚的守护者。她不断地施展自己智慧、心灵和双手的力量，直到四个孩子相继离开，去上中学或大学，然后开拓出属于他们自己的一片人生天地。这是一种长期而又无私的奉献，无偿而又忠诚地奉献给她从未谋面的姐姐的孩子们。

抵达后第一周的日子记忆犹新。这时，我们去的是卫理公会教堂，因为我们自己的教堂正在进行改造和修缮，其面貌一如今日之教堂。

第一周的星期天，我们都去了那间教堂，就位后，座无虚席。牧师从讲坛上下来，走到我们的座位旁，请父亲和他一起证道，父亲接受了，跟着牧师走到前面。

burden, but this young girl, still in boarding school, which she must give up, after that year, for a time, if not always—sixteen or seventeen years of age! Think of our carefree girls of that age now, if they were faced with such responsibility to be laid upon them.—"As thy days, so shall thy strength be", proved true for her, with these unnatural burdens laid upon her.

With fine courage she met them, and was the faithful, efficient and loyal guardian, spending her powers of mind, heart and hands continually; until one after another of the four children were to the ages of going away to school or college, and then making places for themselves in their own niches in life. It was a long, unselfish devotion, given freely and loyally to the children of sister she never knew.

One little memory still persists of this first week. We attended the Methodist church, at this time, as our own church was undergoing alterations and repairs, to produce much the same one which we know in this day.

On that first Sunday, we all went to that church and we filled to overflowing our seat, or seats. The minister came down from the pulpit to our seat, and invited father to take a place with him, which he accepted, following him there. Little "Mousie" always expected to go wherever he went, and she slipped off the high seat and followed too, creating quite a consternation, as he turned at the steps, and found who purposed to be tucked by his side up there! "Mousie" was a very determined little body, and it took some persuading—apparent to the whole congregation, eagerly looking on, and wondering who would be victor. Then the little maid was led back to her proper seat, and he returned to his, and the service opened.

[Third Culture Kids]

Many visitors, quite naturally, came to see us, some with deep, heartfelt interest; some out of curiosity, somewhat as if they were at a circus, and looking at strange specimens. We were beset to talk in the Chinese language, which was far more amusing and wonderful—in the utter ignorance of all things foreign at that time—than in this day. And they laughed at us, we thought, instead of at the odd language, so we ran away and hid on occasions.

I remember crawling as far back as I could get under our bed once, and had to be brought out, because someone in particular wanted to see me. There was a little girl

由于小莫西总是父亲去哪儿她就跟到哪儿，于是，她也从高高的座位上溜下来，跟着走过去，当父亲在台阶上转过身来，发现莫西有意躲在他身边时，给吓了一大跳。小莫西可是个非常有主意的小家伙，一众人等谁都看得出，于是热切地观望着，想知道谁会获胜，父亲说服她颇费周折。最后，莫西被领回座位上，父亲返回到讲台上，礼拜开始了。

【第三文化的孩子】

很自然，有许多访客来看我们，有些人带着深切、由衷的兴趣；有些人是出于好奇，有点像在马戏团看奇怪的动物。让我们困扰的是用厦门白话交谈，当时人们对所有外国事物一无所知，那时讲厦门白话比今天更逗趣，更令人惊奇。我们一讲厦门白话他们就大笑，我们觉得他们嘲笑我们，而不是嘲笑那奇怪的语言，所以我们有时掉头就跑，躲避起来。

我记得我曾经钻到床底下，爬到最里面，最后不得不把我拉出来，因为有人特别想见我。她带来个小女孩，起到了缓和作用。

　　我们四个孩子存心想要尽快忘记厦门白话，只要有可能，就绝不使用它，我们自觉自愿，所以成功地做到了。

　　在最初的日子里，有一件事值得一提。拆箱子拿衣服时发现，从厦门带来的因长途航行没法洗衣而多准备的衣服，有许多从未拆封过，都是用最廉价的印花布做的，打算用一次就扔到船外。其中有些衣服有渍但不脏，被父亲放在一个大帆布袋里，该怎么处置它们呢？

　　有需要的人只管开口就可以拿走的消息流传开来，于是四面八方的电话打过来，这些衣服逐渐送光了。

　　我隐约觉得，我已经是个年轻的女士了，我们的缝纫茶会肯定也强化了这一点；因为我的冬衣上部是抵肩，拼接到腰部打褶，再向下一直开到裙子的底部。这就是当时在厦门的女士们——施敦力小姐⑦、我母亲，还有其他人——的着装方式，有时，她们穿着晨礼服裙袂飘飘，下面是刺绣的衬裙。我想，在这里她们为莫西和我做的衣服，就是这样的！

with her, which was reconciling.

　　We four youngsters deliberately purposed to forget the language as soon as possible, by refusing to use it, whenever possible to avoid it, which we succeeded in doing quite readily.

　　One remarkable condition developed in those first days. The unpacking of clothing prepared, in Amoy, for the long voyage without laundering, revealed a quantity of dresses which had never been unpacked, all made of cheapest print materials, to be used only once and thrown overboard. Also there were articles stained but not soiled, among them, which father had put into a large canvas bag. What was to be done with them all?

　　Word was circulated among needy ones, that these thing could be had for the asking, which brought calls from far and near; and so they gradually disappeared.

　　I had an indefinite idea, which this sewing bee must have quite strengthened, that I was a young lady now; because my winter coat was made on a yoke and pleated at the waistline, but left open to the bottom of the skirt. Now this was the way the young ladies in Amoy dressed—Miss Katie Stronach, and mother, and others—on occasions, in their morning gowns floating open, with embroidered petticoats showing underneath them. And here, I thought, they had made dresses for Mousie and me just like these!

So, after a few days, I—the young lady—with my younger lady sister, came down stairs, hand in hand, in our morning gowns, and our thoughts up in the clouds! After my explanation of young ladyhood, we had it explained that these coats, mine blue and Mousie's a gay plaid, were not dresses to be worn in the house, but coats for out of doors in the cold—they were too warm for the house, and we had to come down to earth as little girls again!

We were soon introduced to school, and found really American boys and girls, not so different from those few we used to know, either.

Back to China

After a year with us, father was urged to return to his work, as before, when he left his two children in this country. The Voice, which always claimed his highest loyalty, led him to lay this request before the grandparents and aunt.

When they consented to his returning for a few years, I think four, he turned his face toward the East again. Strong to endure, as all his course of life showed him, he accepted this sacrifice a second

所以，几天后，我——一位女青年——和我的小淑女妹妹手拉着手，穿着晨礼服，走下楼梯，想入非非，仙气飘飘！在我解释了青春淑女风之后，我们又用自身说明了一点：我的蓝外套和莫西的灰格子外套，不适合室内穿，只适合寒冷的户外。它们在房间里太热了，所以我们又被打回原形，从仙女变回小姑娘。

不久后，我们被领去入学，看见真正的美国男孩和女孩，也发现他们和我们以前认识的那几个美国孩子没有什么不同。

父亲返华

陪我们待了一年之后，父亲被催着回去工作，上次返华他把两个孩子留在美国，这次一样，扔下四个孩子。内心中那个总是呼唤他最大忠诚的声音，使他向外祖父母和小姨妈提出难言的请求。

当他们同意他回去几年，我想是四年，他再次转头朝向东方。他坚强、隐忍，就像他一生所展现的那样，他第二次接受了这种牺牲。他留下的担子不轻，也是巨大的牺牲，做出牺牲的人既是照顾我们的亲人，也是父亲自己。

就在他离开我们之前，他把我们召集到一起，让我们孩子们保证，他一直陪伴我们做的晨祷会继续下去；我们在每天上学前，忠实地做了四年，或者对最年长的查理来说，坚持到他外出求学前。晨祷时，我们每个人都读几段《圣经》经文，依次拿起一本书，然后又挑了另一本书，每个人都祈祷。

要离开自己热爱的祖国，对父亲来说是一个格外艰难的时刻。他于1861年4月离开，就在博雷加德⑧将军在南卡罗来纳州下令炮击北军驻守的查尔斯顿港萨姆特堡⑨，进而打响内战第一枪之后，对于接下来南北双方各州之间悲哀和残酷的战争，他三个月甚至更长的时间里一无所知。除非机缘巧合，也许会有一艘船路过，带来美国的新闻，会有关于这场战争的内容。

到达厦门后，偶尔有机会通过英国或其他国家的船只了解到一些信息。只有通过偶然的方式，他才能知道国内冲突的进

time. It was no light burden he left behind, and a deep sacrifice, accepted by those caring for us, as well as by him.

Just before he left us, he gathered us together and asked us to promise we children would continue the morning prayers he always had with us; which we did faithfully for the four years—or until the oldest one, Charley, went away to school—before going to school in the morning. We each read a few verses from the Bible, taking a book in consecutive order and then selecting another book, and each prayed.

It was a peculiarly trying time for father to leave his beloved country. He left in April, 1861—just after the first gun was fired upon Fort Sumter by Beauregard from Charleston Harbor, S.C.—and of the next moves of the sad and bitter war between the States, he was to know nothing for three months or more, unless by haphazard. Perhaps a vessel might be passing, carrying foreign news from the U.S., and items of this War would be included.

After reaching Amoy, there were occasional opportunities of learning something through British vessels, or other foreign ones. Only by Casual means could he know what was developing in the conflict at home, until finally, budgets of daily papers subscribed for began arriving, three or four months late, in an overwhelming package.

Grandmother's Letter Writing

Letters from grandmother and his older children, written every month, supplementing his information with trustworthy news, so far as possible to give, came regularly also, after the first lapse of time.

I want to write of the wonderful faithfulness and loving kindness of grandmother in connection with these letters. She was intensely interested in all news of the War, in a very intelligent way. A courier brought a daily paper of the latest hour of printing from Morristown (seven miles away) to add to the slower information arriving in evening or late afternoon, of the day before's. A vivid picture, continuing through the four years, rises up, of grandmother sitting at the table, with a candlestick in hand, whose lighted flame, held close to the printed page, moved back and forth across the columns, with lips moving in eagerness, reading the news, and often bowing her head in grief and distress at the awful wreckage of the

展，直到最后，一批批订阅的报纸装在一个巨大的邮包里，开始送达厦门，已然是迟到三四个月的旧闻。

外祖母写信

外祖母和父亲较大的子女每个月都写信，尽可能多地给他提供可靠消息。在最初一段无信的间隔之后，信件定期到达。

关于这些信件，我想写一下外祖母的坚守和慈爱。她对所有关于内战的消息都格外热切，而且是以一种非常智慧的方式关注着。一名信使送来了一份从七英里外的莫里斯敦刚刚印出来的日报，内容是最近一个小时所印刷的新闻，以补充前一天晚上或傍晚到达的慢腾腾的信息。一幅贯穿整个四年的生动画面油然而生：外祖母坐在桌边，手里拿着一盏烛台，燃着的烛火靠近报纸页面，在栏目间来回移动，嘴唇急切地动着，读着新闻，看到痛苦可怕的战争惨景和令人不安的消息，她经常垂首心伤。

在写给父亲的信中，她基于掌握的信息做出明智判断，煞费苦心地把握事件未来发展趋势，并把自己的印象传递给父亲。她不仅自己每个月写信，内容很长，字迹优美，还成功地让孩子们每个月写信，后两年，萨米和小莫西也加入了写信队伍。我们在石板上写第一遍，外祖母把每一份都修改一遍，这样，每封信都写得很像样！然后我们在薄薄的、蓝色或白色的纸上重新抄写一遍，这种纸张当时普遍用于对外通信，但薄到用钢笔写字通常会划出破洞，而且我们在这张薄薄信纸的两面都写了字，这对外祖母和我们来说，是很令人厌烦的事。父亲离开的四年里，我们寄出的就是这样的信。我不记得大家曾忘记写信，父亲也一次不落。有一次，当月的包裹迟到了，最后总算到了，但外包装污黑一片，上面横着盖有指示戳，说一艘英国邮政汽船失事，邮包沉入海底，该包裹是从印度洋海床打捞上来的。

War, and the disturbing news often brought.

In her letters to father, she painstakingly gave him her impression of the forward march of events, with wise judgment gathered from her grasp of them. But she not only gave of herself in long, finely written letters, every month; but she brought about no failure in the children's monthly letters, and in the latter part of the time, Sammy and little "Mousie" also added theirs. We wrote the first copy on slates, and she corrected each one so as to make quite presentable letters! Then we recopied them on thin blue or white paper—used universally in foreign correspondence at that time—so thin, that often the steel pens used, would break through and make holes, and we wrote on both sides of this thin paper, too; a task wearisome to grandmother, as well as to the children. We sent these letters during the four years he was away. I do not remember that they failed him ever, or that he ever failed us. Once the month's package was late; and finally it came to us in a blackened envelope, stamped across with the statement that this package had been brought up from the bottom of the Indian Ocean, when the bed had been dragged for mail which went down in the wreck of a British mail steamer.

[Mail & Doty's Death]

Another exciting incident in connection with our mail was when father was returning to America the last time. He sent a letter just as he was leaving Amoy, which caught a mail ahead of him, stating that the captain of the "N. B. Palmer" had decided to change the course of his vessel to crossing the Pacific to California, instead of taking the usual one through the Indian Ocean.

This proved to be a ruse to put the "S. S. Alabama" off their track, as she was prowling about the China waters (1863-'65) to destroy ships flying the Federal flag! So the "N. B. Palmer" started due east, for California for three days out, then turned southwest, into the Indian Ocean, and so on to America.

In this fourth year, he was ordered by the physician to draw his work to a close and return to his homeland, his health having entirely failed him; but four days before he reached these shores, his spirit entered the new life. We knew the "N.B. Palmer" was daily expected, and watched the papers to catch the first shipping news, before the slow mail coming late in the afternoon

【邮件和父亲离世】

与邮件有关的另一件令人激动的事，是父亲最后一次回美国的时候。就在他要离开厦门时，寄出了一封信，邮件却先于他到达。信上说，"N.B. 帕尔默"号的船长决定改变船只航线，不是像往常那样穿过印度洋，而是改为横渡太平洋到加利福尼亚。

最终证明这是一个诱使南军的"S.S. 阿拉巴马"号战舰偏离航线的计策，因为它1863—1865年间在中国水域巡游，试图摧毁任何悬挂北方联邦旗帜的船只！因此，"N. B. 帕尔默"号朝正东出发，向加利福尼亚航行三天之后，再掉头转向西南，进入印度洋，接着去美国。

第四年时，父亲的健康状况彻底恶化，医生命令父亲结束工作，返回美国。但在他抵达美国海岸的四天前，他的灵魂获得了新生。我们知道"N.B. 帕尔默"号每天都可能抵达，就紧盯着报纸，赶在傍晚慢吞吞的邮班可能会给我们带来信件和信息

帕西帕尼镇上罗畬之墓

might have brought us letters of information. And so word came to us at the close of the shipping paragraph, stating that the "N. B. Palmer" had docked, March 18, 1865, with notice of his death at the end.

His body lies buried in the Cemetery at Parsippany, New Jersey, in the plot where mother would have lain, if she had reached her old home before that event came to her.

Mary Augusta Doty Smith
March 4, 1931

之前，得到最新的航运讯息。我们在报纸航运简讯的栏目末尾看到消息说，1865年3月18日，"N.B. 帕尔默"号已经靠港，结尾处则是父亲的死讯。

父亲的遗体葬于新泽西州帕西帕尼镇公墓，如果母亲在不幸发生之前回到老家，她也会安息于此。

玛丽·奥古斯塔·罗蕾·史密斯
1931年3月4日

【注释】

① 来坦履（Rev. Daniel Rapalje），美国归正会传教士。他于1858年来到厦门，在这里一直工作到1866年的夏天，5月31日离华返美。他补编完成美国归正会传教士打马字的遗稿《厦门音字典》（*E-mng im e Jitian*），这是一部独具特色的闽南方言字典，但打马字没有编撰完就去世了。他死后二年，即1894年，经来坦履牧师补编后，方由厦门鼓浪屿萃经堂刊印。来坦履在序言里引述打马字的一段话来说明编纂此字典的主旨："我多年久有在备办此号《厦门白话的字典》，将中国较常用的字合圣册所有的字解明。我打算此个字典大帮赞信主的人，给伊会学读伊本国的字……无此号字典通看，唐人爱识伊本国的字是难。逐字着跟先生读即会识，自己没会晓用平常的字典。因为平常的字典是着人已经识字即会晓看。……"（按：原文罗马字，今逐音翻为汉字，故必须用闽南话判读）《厦门音字典》用罗马字拼音白话字写成，全书共有469页，字典部占385页，依字音ABC编排，有义解及用例，每字占一行至数行不等。另有字部（部首，第387～392页）、目录（第393～461页）及改错、补录字（第465～469页）。全书共收字数约6378字。其重要价值在于为英国长老会传教士甘为霖（William Campbell）编撰《厦门音新字典》（*A*

Dictionary of the Amoy Vernacular Spoken throughout the Prefectures of Chin-Chiu, Chiang-Chiu and Formosa）提供了蓝本，为美国早期的汉语教学与研究做出了不可磨灭的贡献。——译者注

② 南十字星座，南天星座之一，是全天88个星座中最小的星座，位于半人马座(Centaurus)与苍蝇座(Musca)之间的银河内。星座中主要的亮星组成一个十字形。——译者注

③ 英语中有谚语"if the mountain won't come to Muhammad, Muhammad must go to the mountain"，意思是"山不走来迎，我便向山行""喊山山不动，只能向山行""山不向我走来，我就向山行去""事不迁就人，人就得迁就事"。此处作者把谚语前后颠倒，"Mahomet couldn't go to the mountain, the mountain could come to Mahomet"，指的是作者不能下海洗澡，就用桶打海水来洗澡。正话反说，倒也风趣。典故出自《圣经》：山不来就默罕默德，默罕默德就去就山。有一天，默罕默德带着他的40个门徒在山谷里讲道，他说信心是成就任何事物的关键，也就是说"人有信心，便没有不能成功的计划"。一位门徒对他说："你有信心，你能让这座山过来，让我们站到山顶吗？"穆罕默德对他的门徒充满信心地把头一点，对山大喊了一声："山，你过来！"山谷里响起了他的回音，回声终于消失，山谷又回归宁静。大家都聚精会神地望着那座山，穆罕默德说："山不过来，我们过去吧！"他们开始爬山，经过一番努力，到达山顶，他们因信心促使希望实现而欢呼。——译者注

④《古舟子咏》，塞缪尔·泰勒·柯勒律治(Samuel Taylor Coleridge, 1772—1834)最具代表性的作品。作为浪漫主义时期伟大的诗人之一，柯勒律治的作品并不多，《古舟子咏》是柯勒律治最伟大的诗篇。这些诗表现了诗人奇特的想象力如何驰骋在遥远的海洋和中古的月下城堡之间，立意新颖，感情激荡，想象奇特，语言瑰丽，音律优美，代表了浪漫主义的神秘、奇幻的一面，在技巧上则发掘了诗的音乐美。他还写有一些伤感、阴郁的抒情短诗，表现了诗人不幸的生活遭遇和抑郁的心情。他写有大量的文学、哲学、神学论著，论述精辟，见解独到，在英国文学史上占有重要地位。——译者注

⑤ 伊斯特河，纽约市哈德逊河河湾，将曼哈顿区、布朗克斯区与布鲁克林区、皇后区分隔开来。——译者注

⑥ "晕陆地"症状几乎只出现在真正意义上的疍民（也称连家船民）身上。有资料显示是因为疍民大多出生在海上，且生命中近80%的时间是在海上度过

的。所以当他们住在陆地上的时候，会出现晕船的感觉。英语中 sea leg 指在
行驶的船上保持平衡、不晕船的本领，但没有 land leg 一词，是作者仿拟 sea
leg 杜撰的词。Unsteady land leg 则指晕陆地。——译者注

⑦ 施敦力小姐（Catherine Stronach），是英国伦敦公会女传教士，1846—
1866 年在厦门活动，1866 年病逝，葬于鼓浪屿番仔墓。施敦力家三兄妹与厦
门有着不解的情缘。大哥亚历山大·施敦力（Alexander Stronach），又作施亚
历山大，英国伦敦公会传教士，其夫妇 1846—1870 年在厦门活动。三兄妹中
最小的是弟弟约翰·施敦力（John Stronach），又作施约翰，英国伦敦公会传
教士，其夫妇 1844—1878 年在厦门活动。约翰与亚历山大都有翻译《圣经》
著作，同时办有妇女识字班。1873 年，约翰·施敦力在鼓浪屿乌埭角创办了
福音小学。1949 年后，福音小学改为笔山小学。——译者注

⑧ 博雷加德（Pierre Gustave Toutant Beauregard，1818—1893），美国南
北战争时之南军将领，以其浮夸的个人风格和勇猛但并非百战百胜的战略举
措而闻名。——译者注

⑨ 萨姆特堡，美国南卡罗来纳州查尔斯顿港口一要塞，1861年4月12日南方
邦联军队在此打响了美国南北战争的第一枪。萨姆特堡战略地位重要，北方
联邦军队驻守此间。在连续炮轰34个小时后，联邦军投降。这一要塞的陷落
标志着美国内战的开始。——译者注

附录　族谱中的罗啻

Appendix　Doty in The Doty-Doten[①] Family in America

节选自《美国的多蒂－多滕家族——1620年五月花号上的移民爱德华·多蒂的子孙后裔》。编者：伊桑·艾伦·多蒂，1035页，1897年初版，1984年再印。

（琼·沃尔顿女士[②]提供）

第367号，罗啻：斯蒂芬·霍姆斯·多蒂与菲比·内尔森之子，1809年9月20日生于纽约州的伯尔尼；1836年5月18日，头婚娶克拉丽莎·多利·阿克利，其妻于1806年出生于康涅狄格州的华盛顿，系赫齐卡亚·阿克利与杰迈玛之女。妻子病逝于东印度的婆罗洲。

以下是罗啻的生平梗概，出自一个颇有建树的女儿笔下。

很小的时候，罗啻就把传教视为使命，矢志学习传教，准备去罗格斯学院和新布伦瑞克神学院学习。纽约州伯尔尼市归正

367. ELIHU DOTY, son Stephen Holmes Doty and Phebe Nelson, b. Berne, N. Y., Sept. 20,1809; m., 1st, New York City, May 18, 1836, Clarissa Dolly Ackley, b. Washington, Ct., Dec. 7, 1806, dau. Hezekiah Ackley and Jemima, his wife. She d. Borneo. East Indies, Oct. 5, 1845. He m., 2d, Parsippany. N. J., Feb. 17, 1847, Eleanor Augusta Smith, b. Troy, N. J..July 27, 1823, dau. Hiram Smith and Mary Alien Osborne.She d. Amoy, China, Feb. 28, 1858.

The following sketch of his life is from the pen of one of his accomplished daughters:

Early in life he felt it to be his mission to preach the Gospel to the heathen, and studied for the ministry with that aim in view, being prepared in his studies at Rutgers's College and New Brunswick Theological Seminary. An historical pamphlet of the Sabbath school of the Reformed Church at Berne, N. Y., says: "On November 3, 1832, Elihu Doty, one of our scholars, entered into full communion with this church on confession of faith. In April, 1833, he was recommended as a fit person for the ministry. He graduated from Rutgers's College, 1835, and from the Theological Seminary at New Brunswick, N. J., in 1836."

Quoting from a Manual of the Reformer Church in America: "His first aspirations after missionary life were formed in the Sabbath school. In his studies he was known for his faithful application and excellent scholarship—not showy, but solid—developing excellent judgment and great balance of mind, and winning respect and confidence by his earnest and decided piety. He was somewhat advanced in age when he began his preparation for the ministry, and by the advice of others overleaped two years of his college course.

"His integrity, intellectual and moral, was complete, and no one ever dreamed of questioning his conscientiousness. His missionary ardor was increased by the magnetic presence and contagious enthusiasm of David Abeel." He graduated from the seminary in 1836, being licensed to preach by the Classis of Schoharie. N. Y., in

会安息日学校的校史册上写道："1832年11月3日，我们的一位学者——罗啻——决志牧养）。1833年4月，他被推荐为教士合适人选。他于1835年从罗格斯学院毕业，次年从新布伦瑞克神学院毕业。"

引用一本《美国归正教会手册》中的话：

他第一次产生做事工的志向是在主日学校。在校学习时，他以切实的运用和出色的学识而为人所知。学识拓展了他良好的判断力和缜密的思维能力，他不卖弄聪明，而是脚踏实地，用认真、坚定和虔诚赢得了尊敬和信心。其实，当他准备做教牧时，年龄偏大，所以听从别人的建议，大学课程跳了两级。

他为人正直，品格完美，德才兼备，从没有人想过质疑他的责任心。因雅裨理的魅力和热情吸引并感染了他，使得他的传教热忱与日俱增。

他于1836年从神学院毕业，同年被纽约州斯科哈里长老监督会按立为牧师。同年6月，他即与埃尔伯特·尼维斯③、威廉·扬布拉德和雅各布·恩尼斯一道，在美国归正教会海外差会的眷顾之下，乘船前往爪哇。作为一个与荷兰归正教会同宗同源的教会，他们以为先行立足于此的荷兰政府会对他们的差传活动展现些许兴趣。但是，在9月抵达巴达维亚时，他们既没有发现友好的欢迎也没有保护，最后婆罗洲被指定为他们的活动区域。经过三年在巴达维亚和新加坡令人沮丧的辗转奔波和等待拖延后，于1839年6月19日抵达婆罗洲的三发，结果几个月后，又遇到了更大的失望。尼维斯夫人患了病，十分虚弱，尼维斯先生不得不离开。恩尼斯先生最终证明不适合做传教士。尽管他天资聪颖，但他被解聘了，最终只得离开事工队伍，从而使刚刚打开局面的事业不得不由扬布拉德先生和罗啻先生苦撑下去。

波罗满和汤普森很快也加入了他们的行列。波罗满和罗啻把自己的精力放在来婆罗洲做生意的华人身上；但在三发和坤甸居住了几年之后，事情变得明朗④，如果到华人的母国去传教，他们的工作可以更有效率。于是，他们于1844年前往中国厦门，于6月底抵达中国南方的这个港口城市。

在1836年离开美国之前不久，罗啻与

the same year, and in June he sailed for Java, in company with Elbert Nevius, William Youngblood and Jacob Ennis, under the care of the Board of Foreign Missions of the Reformed Church, which believed the Dutch Government established there would show some interest in the missions of a church whose fathers had come from Holland. But, on arriving at Batavia in September, they found no friendly welcome or protection, so finally Borneo was assigned as their location, and they reached Sambas, Borneo, June 19, 1839, after three years of disheartening labor and delay in Batavia and Singapore, only to meet further disappointments, for, in a few months, Mr. Nevius was obliged to leave on account of his wife's broken health, and Mr. Ennis proved himself a very unfit man. Notwithstanding his mental endowments, he was dismissed and finally deposed from the ministry, thus leaving the work so newly established to be carried forward by Mr. Youngblood and Mr. Doty.

Messrs. Pohlman and Thompson soon joined them, when the former and Mr. Doty devoted themselves to the Chinese who came to Borneo for purposes of trade; but after a few years' residence in Sambas and Pontianak, it became evident they could do more efficient work among the Chinese, if in their

中国推而广之，逐步深入。

　　在生命的最后几年里，罗啻先生非常积极地从事翻译工作，把那些他们认为合适的作品翻译成汉语。前文引用的《美国归正教会手册》提道："令人称羡的是他非常适合这一方面工作，因为他精益求精的习惯，因为他坦率、审慎、自由的精神，他不会心血来潮或偏听偏信。他是勤劳之人，性格中没有虚夸浪漫的成分。他是严格而坚定的劳动者，顽强地持之以恒。面对困难，他展现出平静的英雄主义，而不是退避。他笔译不断，从不停歇，直到朋友们强迫他才辍笔停下。"

　　他的作品有：《翻译英华厦腔语汇》；翻译和修订了《乡训十三则·厦门方言版》，其中收录了米怜的《进小门走窄路解论》；《关于"God"一词汉语译名的一些思考》；《婆罗洲游记》；将荷兰新教归正教会的圣礼和婚姻形式翻译成厦门白话。

　　1858年，在当任领事海雅先生不在时，罗啻先生代理美国领事，他的判断总是明察秋毫、恰如其分，以至于在他的一生中，总有人来征求他的意见和建议。传

of their conversion, and through the course of Mr. Doty's life from this date his was the work of building up that for which he, with his associates in the earlier days, laid the foundation; also the widening of the field and work back into the country...

Mr. Doty was very much engaged during the later years of his life in translations into the Chinese language of such works as were deemed suitable. The "Manual," quoted from before, says: "He was admirably fitted for this department, by his habits of accuracy, his candor, judgment, and freedom from caprice and prejudice. He was a laborious man; there was no romance in his character. A stern, determined worker, he sturdily pressed on. He met difficulties with a quiet heroism, but turned not aside. He never spared himself until his friends compelled him."

His publications were: Anglo-Chinese Manual of the Amoy Dialect, Translation and Revision Into Amoy Dialect of Milner's Thirteen Village Sermons, including Milne's Tract on the "Straight Gate", Some Thoughts on the Proper Term for "God" in the Chinese, Narrative of a Tour in Borneo, Translation of Sacramental and Marriage Forms of Reformed Protestant Dutch Church into Amoy Colloquial.

It was during 1858 that Mr. Doty acted as American Consul during the absence of the appointed Consul, Mr. Hyatt, and his judgment was so clear and just that throughout his life he was constantly sought for advice and counsel. The necessities of a missionary's life tend to develop one's genius in every channel, and in the absence of a dentist Mr. Doty often rendered assistance in that line, and by performing slight surgical operations, while his knowledge of Natural Philosophy often aided others and himself in securing comforts and helps which seemed little short of witchery to the simple natives. His publications were also bound under his supervision and direct aid, the press being in his study. At certain seasons of the year he was a great sufferer from asthma, many times being unable to lie down or rest in any position, while at all times he was never robust. Death entered this fold also, taking the oldest and the then only son, again and later the babe for whom the mother gave her life for, in February, 1858, Mrs. Doty died, leaving the tender mother-father the solicitude of four other little ones whom he brought to the care, so kindly and generously offered, of his wife's parents and sister, in 1860.

After spending one year in this country, recruiting in health and

教生活条件困窘，往往能催生一个人全方位的才能。在没有牙医的情况下，通过外科小手术，罗啻先生常常帮忙修牙；他的自然科学知识经常协助别人和自己获得慰藉和救助，这对简单淳朴的当地人来说几近神乎其神。他的书也一定在他的监督和直接协助下出版，印刷机就在他的书房里。一年中某些季节里，哮喘让他很是遭罪，许多时候根本躺不下，换什么姿势都无法休息，而他的身体也从来都不算强壮。死神还是来到了这个家庭中，带走了老大，也是当时唯一的儿子，后来又带走了那个婴儿，而母亲为了这个婴儿献出了自己的生命。1858年2月，罗啻太太去世了，给慈父慈母留下四个小家伙去牵挂呵护。1860年，罗啻把四个小家伙带回美国，交给了岳父母和妻妹，而他们仁善而慷慨地主动提出照顾孩子们。

在美国待了一年，罗啻一边恢复健康，一边让孩子们开始接受教育，之后他又重新转向毕生为之奉献的差传，继续在华艰辛地工作。历经家国沧桑、教会变迁之后，直至体力明显日渐不支，身体的信号告诉他自己事尽尔。然后，1864年11月30日，他在百感交集中登上返回美国的"N.B. 帕尔默"号快船。当他站在甲板上，告别收养他的家：这片土地上有他几乎全部的人生经历，在这里他与许多人有了关联，在这里他体验到了撼动灵魂的激情，那欢乐深得无法言表，那悲伤"心知其苦"；在他还差四天就到达目的港时，那疲惫不堪的躯体再也无法承载桎梏加身的灵魂，他终于挣脱束缚，与上帝同在，于1865年3月18日安息主怀。他的葬礼在纽约市拉斐特广场的荷兰中心教堂举行，也在新泽西州帕西帕尼的教堂举行。他珍贵的遗骸就安葬在该城的墓地里。

罗啻第一任妻子所生子女：

第752号，长子费里斯·霍姆斯，1838年7月10日出生于新加坡；1844年7月19日卒于中国厦门。

第753号，长女克拉丽莎·伊莱扎，1843年1月14日出生于婆罗洲坤甸。

第754号，次女阿梅莉亚·卡罗琳，1845年1月21日出生于中国厦门；后来由约翰·杜波依斯牧师收养，随其姓氏，住在纽约州的沃茨伯勒。

starting his children in their education, he again turned his face to the work to which he gave himself for life, and continued in arduous labors, through different vicissitudes, national and ecclesiastical, until his gradual but certainly failing physical powers told him his work was done. Then with mingled feelings he embarked on the "N. B. Palmer" for the United States, on November 30th, 1864, and as he stood on her deck, bade farewell to the home of his adoption, the land where he had lived into nearly the whole of his life experiences, where most of his associations were formed, and where he had passed through the deeper passions that stir one's soul, the joys too deep for utterance and the sorrows in which "the heart knoweth its own bitterness;" but within four days of his destination the worn-out body could no longer hold the fettered spirit, and breaking its bonds he was with his God, and at rest, March 18th, 1865. The funeral services were held at the Middle Dutch Church, Lafayette Place, New York City, and also in the church in Parsippany N. J., and his precious remains lie in the cemetery in that place.

Children by Elihu Doty's first wife:

752. i. Ferris Holmes, b. Singa-

pore, India, July 10, 1838; d. Amoy, China, July 19, 1844.

753. ii. Clarissa Eliza, b. Pontianak, Borneo, Jan. 14, 1843.

754. iii. Amelia Caroline, b. Amoy, China, Jan. 21, 1845; was adopted by Rev. John Dubois, and is known by his name; lives Wurtsboro, N. Y.

And by his second wife, b. Amoy, China:

755. iv. Edward Smith, b. Dec. 11,1847; d. July 14, 1848.

756. v. Charles Winchester, b. Nov. 1, 1849.

757. vi. Mary Augusta, b. Sept. 16, 1851.

758. vii. Samuel Holmes, b. Oct 18, 1853.

759. viii. Ellen Marcia, b. Oct. 12, 1855; not m.; lives Summit, N. J.

760. ix, Elmira Louisa, b. Feb. 10, 1858; d. July 2, 1858.

Note from Jean Walton: I have included these pages because the information here conflicts with some in the De Jong history of the China Mission. (I have never seen the whole book—was sent selected pages.)

Bill's note: perhaps another minor error in De Jong: he wrote that Dr. John Otte's son, Frank Otte, was a Colonel, but Frank's

罗啻第二任妻子所生子女（均在中国厦门出生）：

第 755 号，次子爱德华·史密斯，1847 年 12 月 11 日出生，夭折于 1848 年 7 月 14 日。

第 756 号，三子查尔斯·温切斯特，1849 年 11 月 1 日出生。

第 757 号，三女玛丽·奥古斯塔，1851 年 9 月 16 日出生。

第 758 号，四子塞缪尔·霍姆斯，1853 年 10 月 18 日出生。

第 759 号，四女埃伦·马西娅，1855 年 10 月 12 日出生，未婚⑤，住在新泽西州萨米特。

第 760 号，小女埃尔迈拉·路易莎，1858 年 2 月 10 日出生，1858 年 7 月 2 日夭折。

琼·沃尔顿的注解：我之所以把这些页面包括进来，是因为这里的信息与德庸（Gerald F. De Jong）记述的中国差传史有些冲突。（我从来没有见过整本书——只收到寄来的挑选出的几页。）

比尔的注解：也许德庸还有一个小错误。他写道，郁约翰医生的儿子弗兰克·奥特是上校，但弗兰克的女儿、医学博士乔安娜·芬利，坚持认为他是一个陆军少校。

罗嘉后裔埃尔伍德·盖格先生⑥的注解：一位著名的历史学家称，佩里准将从未到过厦门——但玛丽记得他来访过，甚至还给他绣了有交织字母的手帕！

daughter, Joanne Finley, M.D., has insisted to me that he was a Major.

Note from Mr. Elwood Geiger, a Doty descendant: A well-known historian claims Commodore Perry never visited Amoy—but Mary remembers his visit, and even monogrammed a handkerchief for him!

查尔斯·温切斯特·罗啻(Charles Winchester Doty)

玛丽·奥古斯塔·罗窨(Mary Augusta Doty)，摄于1934年

塞缪尔·霍姆斯·罗啻(Samuel Holmes Doty)

埃伦·马西娅·罗奄·约翰逊(Ellen Marcia Doty Johnson)，
与艾尔弗雷德·V. C.约翰逊(Alfred V. C. Johnson)于1885年8月19日
结婚(照片大约于1873年摄于曼荷莲学院)

【注释】

① 罗啻家族姓氏Doty，其拼写并不唯一，读音一般分为两种：['dɔti]和['dɔtən]。例如Doty、Doten、Dotey、Dotte、Doton、Dotin、Doughty、Doughten、Dotee、Dolton、Dowty、Dowtie、Dotten、Douty。其可能的来源有三：英语Doughty、Dotten；法语De La Noye and Doten、Delano and Doty；德语Dotee。美国普利茅斯殖民地的第二任州长威廉·布莱德福（Governor William Bradford），在自己任上30年时出版了《普利茅斯殖民史》（History of Plymouth Plantation）一书，附录中有"五月花乘客名单"。其中有"史蒂文·霍普金斯及妻子伊丽莎白，带着前妻所生两个孩子：儿子贾尔斯，女儿康士坦沙；现任妻子所生两个孩子：达玛丽斯和奥西娜斯，奥西娜斯生于来美国航行途中；还带着两个仆人，名叫爱德华·多蒂、爱德华·李茨特"。史蒂文·霍普金斯先生是皮匠，罗啻的祖先爱德华·多蒂（Edward Doty）是仆人，或者是工人或学徒身份。著名的《五月花号公约》上，也有爱德华·多蒂的签名。其妻子费思·多蒂（Faith Doty）初嫁、再嫁共生有3个女儿，6个儿子，均随原配多蒂的姓氏，儿子全名分别是Edward Dotey、John Douty、Thomas Douty、Samuel Dotey、Joseph Doten、Isaac Dotey（Doughty）。姓氏拼写变化之大可见一斑——译者注。

② 琼·沃尔顿女士，新泽西州邮政史学会秘书，也是《罗啻的花园》的作者，提供了玛丽·奥古斯塔·罗啻（1851—1937）的自述材料，这本八十页的书引人入胜，讲述了她人生之初前八年在厦门生活的故事。

③ 埃尔伯特·尼维斯（Elbert Nevius），美国归正教会的牧师，受美部会委派，他在1836年6月初和夫人一起离开纽约到海外传教。同行的还包括罗啻先生和其他一些传教士。9月，他们抵达巴达维亚，尼维斯在那里停留了一段时间来学习中文。后来他同罗啻一起在婆罗洲工作，但由于健康原因不得不离开。尼维斯曾试过到澳门居住，但这都没能使他恢复健康，于是他在1845年返回美国。回国之后，他担任了纽约州东部归正教会教区的主教。——译者注

④ 事情变得明朗更多是由于第一次鸦片战争以清政府战败告终，丧权辱国，割地赔款，允许洋人来华传教之缘故。——译者注

⑤ 族谱中说埃伦未婚，至少是1897年之前是如此。但是本书作者玛丽提供的照片中说明文字提及，埃伦1855年10月12日出生，与艾尔弗雷德·V．C.约翰逊于1885年8月19日结婚。鉴于作者玛丽是埃伦的亲姐姐，而族谱《美国的多蒂－多滕家族》于1897 年初版时，编者伊桑·艾伦·多蒂可能不知情，玛丽的说法更为可取。

⑥ 南达科他州的埃尔伍德·盖格先生是罗雷的后人，他热心提供了罗雷及家人的照片，并允许使用玛丽·罗雷的故事。玛丽·J.盖格得到一份带手写更正和增补的复写本，并在1972年春天重新打印。